ROCK HARD BODYGUARD

ALEXIS ABBOTT

Get an EXCLUSIVE book, **FREE** just as a thank you for signing up for my newsletter! Plus you'll never miss a new release, cover reveal, or promotion!

http://alexisabbott.com/newsletter

"Joe. Hey, it's me. Listen, we've got a problem. You're not gonna like it, and I think you know what it's about. But I want--Joe, for god's sake, calm down. Joe, I want to help you out, but we don't got a lot of time. Someone's on the way to your house now. As soon as I hang up, get into your car and drive west out of town until you get to the gas station by that billboard with the hole in it. I'll meet you there."

Joe's still stammering out a few panicked words when I end the call and look at myself in the bathroom mirror, seeing the dark rings under my eyes. I brush my hand through my messy, dark hair, then run cold water and splash some in my face and into my short, scruffy beard.

I give myself one more look in the mirror,

wondering if the face about to drive into that Vegas desert is the same man that'll be driving out.

A minute later, I get into my car, give my shitty duplex one last look, and pull out onto the road, the headlights of the convertible being the only light besides the thin sliver of the moon in the sky.

I won't be coming back here.

My rough hand grips the steering wheel tightly as I roar down the desert road, nothing but endless sand and the occasional dried-out shrub on both sides of me. There's no music playing from my radio. No piping-hot coffee in my hand.

Just me and the weight of what's got to happen tonight.

Joe was scared shitless in that phone call. Part of me wonders if he'll listen to me and actually meet me out here. Part of me hopes he doesn't. Hell, maybe that's why I was so curt on the phone, in my subconscious.

The mob wants Joe Mackey dead. He's in deep, deep debt, and they've realized they're never getting their money from him.

In the passenger's seat of my car is a bag full of a week's rations, a forged passport with a fake name and Joe's picture in it, and enough cash to last anyone a nice, long time. It's the perfect package to skip the border and settle down in Mexico in relative comfort. It's the best chance for someone like

Joe to give the mob the slip and start over as a new man.

And in my jacket is the gun I'm bringing to kill Joe Mackey.

The bag is just bait to get his guard down.

I've been an enforcer for the mafia in Las Vegas for a long time. Longer than I'd like to admit. The money and the power I could wield even as just hired muscle would be tempting to any young man growing up in Vegas, but if I could have seen myself now, I wonder whether I would have still started agreeing to security gigs, then debt collection, then extortion. Now murder.

I'm about to cross a line I can't come back from.

I reach the gas station and find that I'm alone. Either Joe hasn't gotten here yet, or he's panicked and fled on his own. I almost wish he has, but that's selfish. It would take his blood off my hands, but he's not a smart enough man to outrun the mob. They'll find him if he's on his own.

I park my car in front of the billboard I told him to meet me at. It's a weathered old thing that hasn't been touched in longer than the abandoned gas station has. It's mostly rust and rotting wood, but the last faded, peeling picture is still up there.

It's a picture of a woman with long, brown hair in a one-piece swimsuit. She's turned so that her ass is facing the viewer, looking over her shoulder with a bright smile that looks downright eerie with all the grime of the years on it. I think it used to advertise the swimsuit company, but there's a huge hole in it toward the bottom where the logo used to be.

While I wait for Joe to show, I stare up at the thing for a few minutes. It always amazes me that some people like the model and the people who run her brand are so close yet so far from the morbid business I'm about to do here.

They just live in this perfect little bubble over everything, never worrying about money, never wondering where the next paycheck or meal will come from, never having to turn to something so dark to survive.

The shine of headlights behind me snaps me out of my thoughts. Damn him, he's coming after all.

It makes it worse knowing that the only reason Joe decided to listen to my offer is that I've known him practically all my life. Mom is a blackjack dealer and dad walked out when I was a kid, so I grew up in and around casinos. And that meant I saw Joe a *lot*. I remember when he only had a few gray hairs, but the Joe I see looking feverish as he brings his car to a stop beside mine is almost bald and starting to go white.

He drank the last traces of his youth away. That's what got him into this mess.

"Wes!" Joe nearly shouts my name as he clambers out of his car, running a hand over his face before running up to me and shaking my hand vigorously. "Oh my god, Wes, I-I-I don't know what to say."

"Don't mention it, Joe," I say, keeping my tone even. "You don't have to explain anything to me."

"Shit, I know," he says, sighing deeply. "I just... I knew you had contacts with these thugs, but I didn't know it would let you see all my dirty laundry like this. You're a good kid, Wes, I hate that you even have an ear to this kind of situation. It was a damn hospital bill when I was young, it put me under so much strain I had to turn to the booze, and the bills just kept coming and I kept drinking and-and-"

"None of that matters anymore, Joe," I say, putting a hand on his shoulder and smiling while I hold back the sadness in my heart. He smiles back at me, and it wrenches a knife into my soul.

"Come on, I'll show you what I've got."

I move to the passenger's seat and pull out the bag, setting it on the hood of the car. I look him in the eye.

"Food. Passport. Money. Your new name is Harold Smith. Skip Mexico City, there should be enough in here to get you all the way down to Merida. I hear it's nice. The drive will be rough, but it's not as rough as what the mob will do."

"Wes..." Joe says, incredible relief on his face, "I...I don't know what to say. Where did all this come from?"

"Don't worry about it. Trade cars with me. This one's clean."

He takes a breath.

"Thank you, Wes. I...I'll never be able to repay you for this."

"I know," I say. "We don't have much time."

"Right," he says, and after a moment's hesitation, he takes the bag, turns, and starts to walk back to the car.

It's a perfect shot.

In a fluid motion, I reach into my jacket and draw my pistol.

He hears it cocking and freezes.

There's a moment of silence between us.

Finally, I break it with a few calm words.

"Get on your knees, Joe."

In disbelief, he obeys, slowly getting down and setting the bag aside before he puts his hands up.

"They...they told you to do it, didn't they?"

"They did, Joe."

I step toward him, gun trained on the back of his head. His hands are trembling. He turns his head ever so slightly, and I can see that his face is pale. "Wes, you don't have to do this."

"It's better this way," I say. "I'll make it quick and clean."

"You don't *want* to do this, Wes," he says, a tremble in his voice. "You're a good guy, Wes."

My jaw sets, and I take a breath, leveling the sights right where I know the shot will be painless.

My finger rests on the trigger, less than a second from that point of no return.

* * *

HOURS LATER, dawn is just starting to break over the desert horizon, painting the sky beautiful shades of blue and pink mixed together.

I'm not driving back to Vegas. I never will again, and I'll never look back to that life. I'm headed west, toward California.

I know how the mafia works. This job was supposed to be a test, and they expected me to come back with news of success, and they'd discuss a promotion for me--something more permanent.

But that's not going to happen. This was the last errand I'd ever accept from the mafia.

By about 6:00 AM, I pull out my phone and call up the one and only contact I have out west.

After a long wait, he picks up the line, and a groggy voice answers.

"...Wes? What the fuck do you want calling at ass-crack o'clock?"

"Cody," I say, my voice gruffer than usual. "I'll buy you breakfast to make up for it. I'll be in LA in about an hour."

"The fuck? Shit, man, what are you coming all the

way out here for?" There's a pause. "You're not drag-ging that shady shit my way, are you?"

"On the contrary," I say, watching the skyline of the city start to come into view, "I'm doing exactly the opposite. I'm calling in that favor you owe me. I need a place to crash until I can get my own place." I take a breath. "...And I'm going to have to find a new line of work."

"*Have a holly, jolly Christmas! It's the best time of the year!*"

No, thank you. I reach out and press a button on the car stereo.

"*Feliz navidad!*"

Double no, thank you. Click. Silence.

"Much better," I murmur to myself, heaving a sigh. I look to my left, through the tinted window of my cherry-red Lexus RX. The beach is virtually deserted, the white sand smooth and undisturbed by footprints.

If you squint and suspend reality just a little bit, you can almost believe it's snow.

But it's not.

Because this is Los Angeles, and even though it is December, the thermometer on my dashboard tells me it's barely less than seventy degrees outside.

Yeah, it's going to be one *those* winters. Most people here love the fact that it never gets too cold, but this December, it would almost be nice if the weather could match my current mood.

I'm driving back from possibly the *second*-most uncomfortable one-on-one meeting I've ever had. I met with my newly-hired lawyer, Arthur O'Connelly, attorney to the stars, to discuss the awful situation I found myself in last week.

I still can't believe this is happening.

I have read in the gossip columns (yes, even I have my weak moments) about many actresses and musicians having to break their contracts suddenly, and the scandals that come to light as a result. It happens so often, I'm actually surprised nobody in my family has gone through it yet.

After all, we are probably the definition of what you might call Hollywood royalty.

My dad, Kenneth Parker, is a semi-retired producer and director. He's made over fifty films during his career and garnered all kinds of prestigious accolades, hosting award shows, being asked to guest-star on variety shows, taking interviews on talk shows. He's well-respected and well-known, a permanent fixture in LA history.

My mom, Pamela Franklin, is an actress with almost the same amount of star power as my father. She's starred in so many movies, she starts to lose count of them, often forgetting which movie was filmed where and when. I can't blame her. My mom is a workaholic to the extreme. Hell, even when she was pregnant with me and then my little sister, she kept working right up until the days we were born.

It bothers me when people say my parents don't deserve what they have. They've worked their asses off to give my sister Andie and me a wonderful life.

And to their credit, they've shielded us from much of the pain and stress of being in the public eye, even despite the many times we've been photographed and editorialized, with or without permission granted. They've always had a pretty tight grip on controlling how much media exposure we got as kids, wanting us to have the most normal childhoods possible, considering the circumstances. I can thank them for not turning me into some bratty, spoiled princess who refuses to work for what she wants.

No, as much as the media would love to portray me that way, I won't let them. Besides, how boring is that? Can these journalists really not come up with a different angle than the whole overdone *"entitled rich girl riding on her parents' coattails"* scenario?

Don't get me wrong, I fully admit that my parents' connections and insider knowledge of the industry has helped me, given me a leg up on the competition. But to make up for it, I do work really hard. My career is everything to me.

I want to be respected not for my famous family

legacy or my last name, but for my talent and ambition. I may be following in my mother's footsteps by becoming an actress, but I refuse to be typecast into the same roles she was. Not because I don't think my mom isn't an incredible actress who has played really cool parts, but because I don't want everyone to constantly draw comparisons between us.

We're two different people, with different talents and interests.

If it isn't already abundantly clear, I really, really don't like when someone slaps a label on me before they even know who I am. People tend to judge me based on my appearance. I understand why. With my thick, mahogany brown waves of hair nearly down to my ass, swimsuit-model body, glittering smile, and big amber eyes, I look like an understudy to a Bay Watch character.

Add to my looks a famous family name and you have a recipe for a gossip-column darling, a favorite of paparazzi and serious journalists alike. I don't know what it is, but people are obsessed with the children of celebrities.

When I was born, the paparazzi staked out the hospital, then our family home in the Hollywood hills. I know my parents were overwhelmed, terrified that overexposure would mess with my head. So they kept a tight watch on Andie and me, tightened their security, threatened legal action against those photographers who got too close and pushed their boundaries. But my parents are also pragmatic. They understood that the public's fascination with their kids was potential source of profit.

So when I was eleven, I posed with my mother for Vanity Fair. I recorded my first commercial for some insurance company when I was thirteen. From there, I springboarded into other minor roles in print and film advertising as well as the occasional part in soap operas.

I've always been interested in fashion, and my mom made sure I was constantly dressed to impress, which paid off--photos of my outfits ended up in magazine features almost monthly. At sixteen, I landed the cover of Teen Vogue. I had a recurring part as the face of a shampoo company for a year or so. At age eighteen, I skipped my senior prom to walk in a fashion show-- closing for one of my favorite avant-garde designers. And in the front row of that fashion show sat a casting director who scouted me for my first major big break-- the lead female character in a dystopian teen drama called *The World Enders*.

Directly after walking across the stage at my high school graduation, I hopped on a plane to Vancouver to shoot the film, in which I played a cheerleader-turned-survivalist who uses her leadership abilities and athleticism to head a group of teens during an apocalyptic war. It was a little over the top, a little cheesy at times, but it was wildly successful. Critics loved it. The public loved it. And ever since I played that role, I have received scripts and offers on a near-daily basis.

It became a lot to sort through on my own, so my parents hooked me up with one of their oldest friends, a fast-talking agent called Eddie Arnold. He's been a friend of the family since before I was born, and I always thought of him as a kind of uncle.

Or at least, I used to.

Anyway, the point is that I have poured my blood, sweat, and tears into my career and my reputation, which is why it's so scary that I'm having to put it all on hold right now.

And it's not even my fault.

I roll my eyes and grit my teeth, forcing myself not to break down and cry.

"Come on, Molly, you're stronger than that," I whisper to myself as I turn the corner and drive up to my cozy condo in Marina del Rey. I parallel-park on the street and, slinging my workout bag over my shoulder, head down the street to my neighborhood gym. This gym is the main reason I pay as much as I do per month for my condo, because it's right up the road.

In my line of work, it's vital that I keep my body in tip-top shape. People don't hire me solely for my skills--at least, not yet. Right now, they hire me because I'm pretty and because my particular style-- my brand--is really hot at the moment. This year, this month, this day, I am exactly what those Hollywood executives are looking for. When I walk into a casting room, I can see faces light up at the sight of me. I am the answer to their questions.

I know this probably makes me sound a little arrogant. Too full of myself. But trust me, there isn't a single part of my existence I take for granted. I know how lucky I am to have inherited my father's wealth and prestige along with my mother's beauty and talent. But my competition is often just as rich, beautiful, and skilled as I am. I need to have the edge. That one thing that makes me stand out, makes me more valuable to the crew.

And I'm already establishing that edge. I do my own stunts.

In *The World Enders*, I had to perform all kinds of jumps, rolls, sprints, and fight choreography. Originally, they offered to hire a stunt double for me. After all, pretty much every one of my co-stars had a double. But I was determined to make myself totally invaluable, irreplaceable in every way.

I've been running track and doing gymnastics since I was a little girl, and for the past few years I've added another workout to the mix: self-defense classes. And I don't mean those wimpy "hit your assailant in the nose and run away" self-defense classes. I mean stuff like taekwondo and krav maga. Like boxing.

I know how to make a fight look real, because I

know how to really fight. Of course, I've been lucky enough to avoid ever having to be in a real fight. But I would like to think that if I had to, I could.

As I walk into the gym and head straight for the treadmill, a sad thought occurs to me.

I may be a fighter trained in self-defense, but even that knowledge couldn't protect me from what Eddie Arnold did to me. I can feel tears burning in my eyes. I shake my head and blink rapidly, refusing to shed a tear over that awful pig of a man.

I step onto the treadmill and instantly turn the speed up as high as it goes. I'm not even in the mood to stretch first. I just want to sweat and run and let my anger motivate me to work harder.

I glance up at the flat-screen television on the wall and am only half-surprised to see the image of my mother's face. I have my earbuds in, listening to my workout playlist, but I can read lips and context clues well enough to figure out that the TV is playing some sort of celebrity gossip show. Cartoon hearts appear around my mother's face on the screen and I smile, a little sadly.

The media almost never has anything bad to say about my mom.

My parents are both hard workers with hearts of gold. I determine after a minute or so that the host of the gossip show is talking about how my mom recently donated a bunch of money to a cancer research organization. She had a breast cancer scare about five years ago, and while it turned out totally benign in the end, she still walked away with an even deeper respect for the victims of cancer and the doctors who treat them.

Good people. My parents are good people. And they only ever associate with other good people, having high standards for who they work with and hang out with on their down time.

But even good people make bad choices sometimes, I think to myself.

Like Eddie. Eddie Arnold is a bad choice. A bad guy.

I swallow hard, feeling sick to my stomach as the memories of this past week flood back to me. The escalation of his attacks, evolving from minor annoyances to genuine harassment to bonafide threats. At first there were just some voicemails left on my phone, urging me gently to call him back so we could talk it out, discuss what happened and come to a congenial agreement about it.

Then there were the texts. Alternating between begging for forgiveness and threatening to "make my life hell" if I didn't return his calls and meet with him.

I ignored them all for as long as I could, thinking eventually he would give up and leave me alone.

All this time, I had no idea just how bad it would get.

I thought at first maybe I could just pretend it

never happened. Pretend I wasn't that affected by what he did. I told myself maybe I misinterpreted his actions. Misread the situation. Exaggerated it in my head. The first couple days, that's what I told myself.

But then, when I thought about it more, I just felt so angry. So hurt. Offended that this man who I've known my whole life, who has been like an uncle to me, could try and take advantage of my trust in him that way. The more he harassed me, the angrier I got. The more I ignored him, the angrier *he* got. Soon, I was getting messages on social media. My Facebook account, my Instagram page, even on Snapchat. I had to turn off my email notifications because he was sending me messages there, too. I figured if I ignored him he would eventually stop, and I could just move on.

But then I realized just how badly he'd tricked me.

Eddie was my go-to guy whenever I needed to sign a contract of any kind. I would have him read through it. He sorted through my offers and scripts, giving me advice. And at some point, he put a contract in front of me to sign. I did. And in that contract, I signed away all the rights to my own career. All my scripts and offers, all my profits. They go through him.

He is holding my career hostage. And that's why I ended up talking to Arthur O'Connelly, attorney to the stars, today. To discuss what steps I should take to break that contract and win back my life from Eddie Arnold.

Arthur didn't mince his words. He told me, straight-up, that this will be an uphill battle. That Eddie is a seasoned veteran in the world of legally binding contracts, and he knows all the loopholes, all the ways to trap me and make me his little marionette.

I finish my workout and walk back home as the sun sets over the beach. I pass by the little eat-in table in my kitchen and at the sight of it, my stomach turns. I flash back instantly to that fateful night last week when my life turned upside down.

It was just a business meeting, or so I thought. A little late in the evening, sure, but Eddie's a night owl, so no huge surprise there.

We met at an upscale restaurant downtown, near closing hours. We were the only people still dining in that late, and Eddie seemed a bit off from the moment we sat down to talk. He sat next to me in the booth instead of across from me. He was slurring his words, but only slightly. He had the top three buttons undone on his silk shirt, the sleeves of his jacket rolled up. Eddie's in his mid-forties, a paunchy, broad-shouldered chain-smoker with a raspy voice and a way of talking so quickly and confidently that he can make anyone agree to almost anything.

He downed three glasses of wine at dinner, while I slowly sipped one. He was telling me all about this new project his director buddy is working on, about how I could be a perfect fit for the lead role. I excitedly told him I was interested, of course, but then he shook his head.

"Yeah, oh yeah, you would be a great fit. Perfect. You got the body for it, obviously," he slurred, gesturing with his hands in the shape of an hourglass. A little inappropriate, maybe, but I ignored it.

"So can you set me up for a casting call?" I asked.

Eddie looked at me long and hard. Then he said quietly, "Yeah, sure can, Molly-pop... But uh, he might need some coaxing."

"Oh?" I asked, frowning in confusion.

"Or rather... I might need some coaxing," Eddie said in a low voice.

And that's when I felt it.

His hand. His meaty, thick fingers sliding up my thigh under the table. I froze up, paralyzed with shock. Eddie gave a low growl and leaned over, his boozy breath hot on my neck. Goosebumps prickled up on my skin. What the hell is he doing? I thought to myself.

His lips brushed my neck, his hand resting on the soft mound between my thighs.

Finally, my shock wore off and I jumped up, sliding out of the booth so quickly that I knocked over our wine glasses and sent a basket of ciabatta rolls flying off the table. I gave Eddie a horrified look and muttered, "What the fuck is wrong with you?"

And then I turned on my heel and ran. Right out of the restaurant. Right into the middle of the street. Cars honked and swerved to avoid me. I hailed a cab and *climbed inside, shaking so hard I could barely tell the driver my address.*

When I got home, I called my sister, sobbing. Andie came over and held me while I cried and told her the whole horrible story. I made her promise not to tell our parents. Not yet. I needed to think it over first. I knew it would be difficult to tell them. Eddie has been their closest friend and confidante for decades. It would be a huge shock to them, that kind of betrayal.

I sit down at the kitchen table and finally allow the tears to fall. But only for a minute or so. Then I wipe my eyes, get up, and murmur, "That's enough. Time to make dinner. Think about something else for awhile."

Just as I'm chopping vegetables at the kitchen counter, I hear a loud, curt knock at the front door of my apartment. I glance at the digital clock on the microwave.

Nine-oh-five.

Not super late, but definitely late enough to arouse my suspicion. I don't have plans with anyone, to my knowledge, and the only person who ever comes over unannounced is my sister Andie. I set down my chopping knife, then think twice and pick it back up as I walk quietly over to the front door. I peek through the tiny peephole.

Nobody there. Empty hallway.

Then I hear a crinkling sound under my foot. I look down to see a white envelope poking out from under my slipper. Scowling in confusion, I reach down and pick it up. It's totally blank. Should I even open it? What if it's--

"No," I sigh. "Come on, Molly. It's not anthrax."

With my heart pounding, I open the envelope and pull out a single sheet of crisp white printer paper. I unfold it to read a brief message in all caps.

COME BACK OR I WILL DRAG YOU BACK.

"Christmas Eve is just a bitch, isn't it?" Cody says as I finish the glass of beer in front of me.

"Enough to drink to," I reply gruffly.

The two of us are having a drink over what we call a lunch break at the bar down the road from my office. I don't usually day-drink. Not on a weekday, at least. But on a day like today, I couldn't turn down an invitation from Cody, because I've got my share of things to drink over.

The two of us are about the same height--a few inches over 6ft--and we have about the same broad, muscled frames, meaning our two bodies take up a hell of a lot of space at the bar. We almost blend together. For Cody, that's a good thing.

Cody's famous. He's LA famous, in fact, one of the biggest up and coming faces on the music scene since the last big thing. Even though it's relatively dim in the bar, he's wearing a beanie, thick-rimmed glasses that are just for show, and a jacket with a collar that makes it easy for him to keep a low profile if he needs to. He looks a little more hipster than my dusty leather jacket, flannel, and jeans, but that just makes me the sore thumb sticking out.

He needs to go a little incognito for meetups like this. The bartender here knows us both, so it's not a huge deal, but he likes to be careful. That, and I think he kind of likes feeling like he has to be careful. He's always had a flair for theatrical shit.

That's how his band got discovered all those years ago when we were still a couple of mob thugs in Vegas together. Never thought I'd owe my new life to this rock star, but there could be worse people, that's for damn sure. I don't think I'll ever get used to hearing Cody the punk I saved from a fight in an alley suddenly doing things with a guitar over the radio I didn't know were possible.

Even with Cody's disguise and us looking like we're looking for a fight, there's a burly, stout guy sitting in the corner of the bar who's been eyeing us since we walked in. I can't tell if he recognizes Cody or if he has beef with me, and as long as he doesn't bother us, I don't care to find out.

"This is the same bar we were at last Christmas Eve, wasn't it?" he muses, turning over the amber beer bottle in his hand thoughtfully.

"Don't," I say with a warning tone and a gruff smile to him.

"Just sayin'," he says, returning it, "you make this a tradition and you're on a steady path to becoming something like a... a depressing regular."

I roll my eyes.

"Seriously though," Cody says, "I didn't set you up with that office down the road so you could drink yourself into an early grave."

"You set me up in *that* office because you want me dead," I say, taking the second round the bartender sets in front of us. "I swear they didn't get all the asbestos out of it the first time."

"Hey, I didn't exactly have time to scope the place out," he says with a chuckle. "You gave me enough prep time to throw a pair of pants on when you rolled into town." He finishes his own beer and looks at me. "You still haven't told me what that day was all about. I mean, don't get me wrong, but I've known you a long time, Wes. I haven't seen that look in your eyes in..."

"Not the time, Cody," I grunt, downing a third of the beer pointedly. "That's a conversation for 2 AM in Tijuana, not 1 PM at Burt's," I say, giving a respectful nod to Burt, the bartender. "Besides, Christmas Eve drinking is for something else."

Cody screws up his face like he's wracking his brain trying to figure out what I'm talking about, and finally, realization hits him. "Ohhh, your dad. Shit. Sorry."

I do a little mental counting. "That's...twelve years now and counting. Fitting for Christmas." Twelve years ago today, that asshole walked out of our house and never looked back. So I never looked back either. Doesn't mean I can't drink to it, though.

Cody tilts his beer to me, and we clink bottles ruefully.

"Might be a little less sour if you'd take on a few of those jobs I know are coming your way," Cody adds, and I shoot him a look.

"None of what's coming my way is really my scene," I say.

"Keep turning down jobs at the rate you are, and I'll start to assume being able to afford food isn't your scene either," he snorts.

"Look, would you do a show at..." I pause, trying to think of an example. "I dunno, a kid's birthday party?"

"That's not the same thing," Cody says. "Exact opposite, actually. Wes, you're one of the best free-lance personal bodyguards on this side of LA, espe-cially for how short a time you've been in the city. You've got a reputation. And celebrities are starting to *throw* work at you, especially around the holidays. You're only in a dry spell because you aren't taking up any of the offers coming your way. The bait's there, why aren't you biting? Most people like you would kill for those kinds of jobs."

"You make it sound like I'm more of a diva than you, rock star," I say in a low tone with a cocky smile, and he ribs me with his elbow before I continue. "You know I don't like all this glam and glitzy shit, man. The kinds of people asking for security were born choking on silver spoons. I did one of those gigs once, and it was some spoiled brat with a trust fund who had a theater career practically handed to them before they'd been born."

"Exactly," Cody laughs, "what's wrong with taking their money?"

I frown.

"Well, it might be worth putting up with it, but then there's all the strings that come attached with celebrity work. Paparazzi. Tabloids. Drama. I don't know how you put up with it all."

"Money is good, my friend," Cody says simply. "The attention isn't bad either. No such thing as bad PR." I know he's right, in some ways.

"That works for you, but there are the other strings attached that only us bodyguards get to deal with when we're not getting paid," I say. "Like the one coming toward us, for example."

Cody looks in the direction I gesture with my finger from my beer, and we watch the burly guy across the room striding toward us.

I recognize him, now. He's the ex-husband of that

theater brat. I'd been hired to protect her during the divorce proceedings.

"Wes Jameson?" he demands, his brow knit.

"I'm off the clock," I grunt, trying to brush the guy off--not that I don't know that'll just antagonize him. Hell, maybe I'm in the mood for a fight today.

"You son of a whore," he says as Cody and I turn around to face him, exchanging a glance, silently agreeing how to handle this when it turns rough in a few seconds. "That bitch took everything I had!"

"I wasn't her lawyer, pal," I say matter-of-factly, and it's true. "All you're doing here is making a mistake."

"Oh bullshit, all of you were conspiring against me," he slurs, and I can tell the guy's been drinking already. I would feel bad for him, if he hadn't cheated on his wife with her mother and gotten violent with both of them. "I saw the looks she gave you. Did you screw that lying bitch, too?"

"No, but you've got a few things wrong there," I say, standing up and looking down at the man. "It wasn't my job to know details, but the way I heard it, you were the one who cheated on her--and buddy, with her looks and your personality, I'm surprised she stuck with you as long as she did."

Yeah, I'm definitely looking for a fight. And now I've got one.

Red-faced, he slings a meaty fist at me blindly. This guy's shorter than me, but the extra weight means he's not someone to underestimate. Fortunately, I've dealt with this guy before. I've physically held him back before, in fact, so I know how much force is behind that punch.

I roll out of the way of the fist and catch him by the wrist. A drunk's main weakness is his reflexes, obviously, so it's the easiest thing in the world to use that against him. With his wrist in my hand, I sidestep him and pull his wrist along with me, using his own momentum against him.

He's surprised, and he stumbles. But a drunk also doesn't think fast enough to panic, so even as he's off balance, he throws another punch at me.

I catch it.

I like this bar, and I'd rather not send teeth flying across its floor, so I deliver a quick, strong knee right into his gut that knocks the wind out of him. I hear him wheeze hard, and that's enough to tell me he's done.

With a solid thrust, I send him stumbling backward and onto the floor, coughing.

I glance back at Cody and see that he's already putting money on the bar with a boyishly apologetic smile to the bartender, who doesn't look either angry or happy, as always.

"We settled?" I ask him, and Cody nods.

"Think it's time we headed out. See ya next time, Burt."

The bartender nods to us, glaring down at the

man on the ground who looks like he's about to throw up as we make our way out the door.

"Man, that just makes me miss our times running security back in Vegas," Cody says wistfully as we step out into the cool winter air. It's LA, so it's not exactly bitter cold, but it's enough for a jacket.

"Trust me, you don't miss it that much," I say with a gruff laugh as we shake hands. "There's easier ways to get that out of your system if you're just hungry for a fight."

"I'll take that as an invitation to kick your ass someday," he says with a wink. "Just like old times."

"We'll see about that," I say with a laugh. "Merry Christmas, asshole."

He throws me the middle finger as he walks away, and I grin, heading the opposite direction back to my office.

It's a short walk, which makes it a miracle I'm not an alcoholic. The building I'm in houses a handful of other small businesses. They're nothing fancy, and like you'd expect from a place where a bar is just a short walk away, it's not the fanciest part of town, but it's not exactly rough either. Sure, there's graffiti on the side of the building, and maybe a window or two needs changing, but it's comfortable.

I head up to my office and find a few letters shoved through the mailbox as I step inside.

The office is cramped. It's about half the size of a studio apartment, which is all the space I need. I keep it tidy and simple--there's a desk, a few drawers for papers, and everything else is electronic. LA is big about the "carbon footprint" thing. A little hard to get used to for someone from Vegas, but I've come to like the space it saves.

I pick up the now-cold coffee on my desk and drink from it as I thumb through my mail. It tastes like shit, but it chases the beer well enough.

And it gives me something besides the mail to frown at.

It's more offers for work from the annoyingly stereotypical Hollywood crowd. I have to admit, it felt good to turn down a few of those offers when I was first on the rise here in LA. Now, though, I have to admit, the work is coming in a little less often.

I set the coffee down and pull on the string of the window blinds, letting light flood my office as I stare out onto the street. Less light than usual.

There's not much of a view anymore. Recently, a massive billboard went up on top of the buildings across from me, stretching across three rooftops and blocking out most of the sunlight. There's a massive picture of some famous actress on it, her cascade of dark hair taking up half the picture, shining bright and artificial in the picture that's advertising a shampoo brand. It could be a worse sight. She's gorgeous, with amber eyes, fuller lips than I've ever seen on anyone in my life, and tall as you'd expect a stunning model to be--presumably not the 50ft or so the billboard is. The name "Molly Parker" is stamped in fancy golden cursive writing under the brand name. A big, glitzy name blown up in my face all day, belonging to some spoiled brat who's raking in cash for looming over the street.

People like that are exactly why I cringe at the idea of working for them.

I toss the envelopes into the trash. It feels like being between a rock and a hard place. On the one hand, the Hollywood scene makes me sick, but Cody's got a point. If I want to stick around LA, I've got to bite the bullet and play their games.

Because the idea of going back to Vegas makes me want to break out the bottle of whisky under my desk.

My personal cell phone buzzes.

I pull it out of my pocket and look down to see Cody's name. Furrowing my brow, I wonder if I accidentally took his card or something as I answer the call.

"Miss me already?"

"Fuck you," Cody says. "Hey listen, Wes, I just got off the phone with one of my friends who's got ties with a studio working on a big A-list movie right now. Heard something you might be interested in."

I roll my eyes. He heard about a job. Despite being in music, Cody still has an ear to the goings-on of the Hollywood celebrity scene, so every now and then, he tries to toss a job my way. I should have known.

"You know I've got a voicemail for junk calls, right?"

"Ha ha," he says in a flat tone. "Look, I know it's not exactly work hours, but that's why you'll want to hear about this one. It's Christmas Eve and this client needs someone ASAP, *tonight*. Like, immediately, and what they're offering in pay shows that."

I raise an eyebrow, take a breath, then step to the window and glare at the billboard before saying, "Alright, you've got my attention. What's the job?"

I listen to Cody rattle off the information, and as I hear the details, my eyes go wide, and not just because of the *huge* paycheck being waved under my nose. I hear the name of the client.

"You've gotta be fucking kidding me," I say.

MOLLY

I stare out the window of the car Arthur hired for me, watching the palm trees of the boulevard pass by under a clear blue sky. There's not a single cloud in sight, the sun beaming down like the world is just a perfectly happy place. Like I should be happy. Like I should be getting ready to celebrate another gorgeous Los Angeles Christmas with my family.

It's Christmas Eve, and instead of heading over to my parents' massive mansion in the Hills, I'm rolling down the road with a strange man chauffeuring me away from my own home, away from the place where I feel safe. Or, at least, the place where I *used* to feel safe.

Andie squeezes my hand.

"Hey," she says softly, trying to get my attention. "Molly, what are you thinking about? You okay?"

I turn and give my little sister a faint, probably unconvincing smile. I'm a great actress, but when it comes to Andie, I can't even come close to telling a lie. She knows me way too well. She can see right through my attempts to brush off her concerns. She tilts her head to one side and clucks her tongue sympathetically.

"I know. This sucks," she sighs. Then, she adds, "Okay, it super-duper sucks. But at least you're taking the appropriate steps to protect yourself, Molls. You're doing exactly what they say you're supposed to do in a situation like this."

I raise an eyebrow bemusedly.

"What *they* say? Who are *they*?"

Her pretty face splits into a big grin and she shrugs. "I don't know. Cops on TV shows."

"Ah, okay. Never let anyone tell you there's nothing to be learned from watching TV," I remark. She giggles.

"So," she begins again, leaning close and lowering her voice to a whisper. Her eyes flick up to the partition screen between the chauffeur and us. "Who is this guy? Like, where the hell did he come from? He looks like a secret agent or something."

And I have to kind of agree with her on that. The driver is wearing all black, a black newsboy cap tugged down over his forehead, casting his face in shadow. He's barely said a single word to me, and I don't know his name. Such is my life now, I guess.

"I don't know. He's just some guy my lawyer hired," I tell her, shrugging.

Andie waggles her eyebrows at me. "Oh, your *hot* lawyer? What's his name again?"

I narrow my eyes and shake my head.

"His name is Arthur. And no."

"No, what?"

"Just no."

"Come on, Molly, he's a little hot."

"Andie," I groan, rolling my eyes, "he's almost Dad's age."

"So? Dudes don't just stop being hot once they hit fifty, you know," she laughs, poking her tongue out at me. I heave a sigh, trying not to smile. I know what she's doing. Trying to distract me with dumb stuff to keep my mind off of the whole ex-agent-stalker situation.

"I don't think Arthur was ever hot, Andie. Not in this decade, not in the last decade, either. You just like him because you're going through an 'older man' phase or whatever," I tell her, elbowing her gently in the ribs. She gives me a faux-scandalized look.

She over-dramatically flips her hair over one shoulder and says, "It's not a phase, Molly. It's just who I *am*."

"Oh my god. Save it for the audition room," I can't help but laugh. She looks pleased with herself for getting me to smile. I know that was her plan all along. She's a really good sister, always making time for me no matter how busy we both are. When we're both in town, we meet up at least once or twice a week for brunch or a movie night at my condo. But even when we're not in the same place at the same time, we Skype at least once a week, no matter what time zones we're each in.

In Hollywood, it can be difficult to make friends, and even harder to keep them. It seems like every girl I meet and click with turns out to be competing with me at the next audition or just trying to befriend me on the off-chance that we might be photographed together for some tabloid.

I try not to take it personally. It's a dog-eat-dog world out here in LA, and everyone here is scrambling for some way to claw their way up the ladder of fame and fortune. I know what I look like to those young women fresh off their Greyhound buses on their search for stardom.

I look like a fast pass to the top. I look like an escalator while everyone else is sweating their way up the stairs. Being dubbed my best friend in the media is like winning the Hollywood lottery. Everyone wants to be my friend--at least until they realize how busy and ambitious I am, how rarely I'm free to meet up with people for fun.

They also tend to figure out pretty quickly that despite what the tabloids would have you believe, I'm actually an extremely private person. My parents instilled that in me from a very young age. They taught me about how dangerous and toxic the world of showbiz can be if you're not careful.

This shiny golden monster called fame is a double-edged sword.

On the one hand, when you're a household name, the offers come rolling in from every direction. You never have to introduce yourself to casting directors. They already know who you are, where you come from, what your pedigree is.

On the other hand, the media scrutiny is unavoidable. Sometimes, it can feel like you're living in a fishbowl, with faces staring in on you at all times, watching your every move, analyzing every word you say, ripping apart your life choices from who to date to the designer you wear. It can be pretty isolating.

Luckily, Andie is my built-in best friend. She grew up the same way I did, surrounded by all the trappings of being Hollywood royalty and what that means--the good and the bad.

She was there when the paparazzi snapped photos of me sharing my first kiss with a boy I met at camp when I was fourteen. I cried on her shoulder when the tabloids called me a slut at that young age, made me ashamed of who I was--a perfectly normal adolescent girl just trying to live a normal life.

Andie was the one who went with me to my first major red carpet event, the premiere of *The World Enders*, right after my longtime-high school sweetheart dumped me and left me to walk the red carpet alone.

The two of us, Molly and Andie Parker, Hollywood princesses in glittering red and gold gowns, respectively, posing for the cameras with our arms linked. The media loved it. They spun all kinds of stories about us. Our names stayed in the headlines for weeks. The fashion police picked and pulled at our ensembles--some calling us overly ostentatious, too stuck up, and others calling us beautiful, poised.

Parker Sisters, Best Friends For Life! proclaimed one headline. And for once, the media got it right. Because we are best friends for life. Sure, when we were little we used to argue from time to time, just like any other pair of siblings. But these days? We're each other's emergency contacts on medical forms. We have each other on speed dial. We even have a special "SOS" code we can send to each other via text that means something serious has happened and we need to talk ASAP.

So it makes perfect sense to have Andie riding along with me today, holding me down and keeping me sane while my world crumbles down all around me.

"Speaking of the audition room," Andie begins, biting her lip in that way that tells me she's about to embark on a tricky topic.

My heart sinks. I knew I shouldn't have said anything about auditions. It's still a bit of a sore subject between us. Andie is just as stubborn and ambitious as I am, and even though she's only eighteen and still in her senior year of high school, she has her mind set on jumping headfirst into acting.

I know it sounds hypocritical, but that's the last thing I want for her. Just because I did it and haven't totally crashed and burned yet doesn't mean it's a good idea for everyone. Especially for Andie. She's smart as a whip, but she's not as cynical as I am. She's too optimistic. She sees the best in everyone, the good outcome of any situation.

"You know how I feel about that, Andie," I tell her gently.

She sighs.

"I do know. But Molls, I'm eighteen. And by the time you were eighteen, you were already neck-deep in work."

"Yeah, exactly. I know what it feels like to be that young and have your freedom and youth stolen away from you," I explain.

"But look how it turned out! You got that big movie and all those offers came your way and it's all working out just fine," she protests.

"Andie," I start, shaking my head. "Look at how my life is going right now. I'm being transported in secret from my condo to some random hotel because my agent, a man we all thought we could trust, has now become some crazy jealous stalker. Clearly, things did *not* work out."

"That has nothing to do with your career, though, Molls. That is not your fault. Eddie is just… Eddie. He's the one who messed up here, not you," she says.

I take a deep breath and put an arm around her.

"That's what I'm saying, sis. You can be super careful and work super hard and do everything right and still have things blow up in your face. My career is ruined. I can't work, I can't do anything until Arthur gets this shit sorted out and wrestles my contract back from Eddie's grimy hands. Look, you think I'm smart, right?"

She nods.

"And you think I've done everything I can, right?"

She nods again.

"Okay. And that's true. But in the end, it's not up to me. It's fate. Sometimes things go well, like with that movie I did. But in this business, when something goes badly… it goes *very* badly. You know what I mean?" I ask.

Andie looks at me for a long moment, weighing my words. Then she sighs.

"Yeah. I know. You're right," she admits.

"It's not that I don't want you to follow your dreams, I just want you to wait a little longer. At least until after you graduate. I never got to go to prom. I want you to have that memory that I don't have," I say, giving her a one-armed hug.

"Okay, okay. Enough with the lecturing," Andie says, her bouncy personality returning instantly. "So, like, what are you gonna do about the family Christmas party?"

My stomach flip-flops. Oh god.

"Uh, I-I'm not sure. I mean, I obviously can't go. Arthur said my safety is a genuine concern right now, and it would be foolish for me to put all of you in danger by going to the party," I explain, my heart heavy. "Eddie either has a lot of time on his hands or a lot of friends in low places willing to do whatever he asks them to do. You saw that massive stack of paper on my desk in the living room, right?"

"Yeah."

"That's all the stuff he's been sending me. Print-outs of the text messages, the emails, the Instagram and Snapchat messages, transcripts of the voicemails he's left me, letters he's been sliding under my door--you name it," I say, feeling that now-familiar prickle of fear in my gut.

"Jesus," Andie breathes, shaking her head. "He's fucking bananas."

"I know. I keep wondering what happened. Where I went wrong. Has he always been this way and we just never saw that side of him? Or did I--I don't know--do something to make him turn this way?" I muse out loud. Andie squeezes my hand.

"Hey. No. Don't you dare blame yourself for what that sick prick is doing. You didn't make him do any of this. He made the decision to be an asshole all on his own. He's a grown-ass man, Molls. Don't take on any of that blame," my sister says fiercely, her brown eyes flashing.

I smile reassuringly. I don't want her or anyone else getting all worked up on my behalf.

"So anyway, the Christmas party. Here's what I need you to do," I begin.

Andie's eyes get wide and I can tell she's afraid of what I'm about to ask.

"I need you to do me a huge favor, Andie. I need you to lie to Mom and Dad."

"Oh, god. Do I have to?" she asks, a pained expression on her face.

"Make up some cover story for me. Tell them I'm working on a motion picture up in Vancouver or something. Shooting a commercial in San Francisco. I don't care. Just, don't tell them I'm hiding out in a hotel instead of going to the party. Please?"

"Molls, you know I haven't told our parents that big a lie since you and I sneaked out to that garage band concert, like, three years ago. Remember? We were grounded, but you convinced me to climb out the window and ride our bikes down to the venue?"

"Uh, actually, it was your idea," I correct her, lifting an eyebrow. "And you were the one who was grounded, not me. And I didn't even like that band."

"Details, details," Andie says, waving her hand dismissively. "Doesn't matter. Either way, I may have gotten the acting gene, too, but I'm terrible at lying to Mom. She can tell immediately. I swear she can read minds."

"Well, then, lie to Dad instead."

"You know what I mean, Molls. For real." She fixes me with an intense stare and adds, "Why don't you just tell them the truth?"

My shoulders slump. I was hoping to just gloss over this whole deal.

"Because, well, my conversation with them about what happened… it didn't go well."

Andie frowns, confused.

"What do you mean?"

"Like, as in, they didn't believe me."

"Didn't believe you? About what?"

I roll my eyes.

"About what happened with Eddie. They just brushed it off. I don't think they really understood what I was telling them. Or maybe they didn't want to understand."

"You mean, they sided with Eddie?" Andie clarifies, that venom seeping back into her voice as her cheeks flush pink with anger.

"No. Yeah. Well, not exactly. It's more like they just couldn't process what I was saying to them. Like they just couldn't compute it in their heads. I mean, I get it. They've known Eddie since before we were born. He's, like, their best friend. They trust him," I explain.

Andie's mouth has set into a hard line.

"That's not fair, Molls. That's fucked up."

"I know, I know. And I'm sure if I could talk to them again in person, explain myself in more detail, they would probably come to terms with it," I say. "But right now, it just isn't safe for me to go hang out with the fam. Arthur was very clear about that. I need to be in hiding."

"So, what am I supposed to do? Just pretend like everything is normal?" Andie asks.

I nod firmly. "Yes. Exactly. When Arthur and I get a better handle on this whole situation, then we'll have time to talk it out. But right now, we just need to get past this hurdle."

"You're gonna be all alone on Christmas," she says softly, and I can tell she's close to tears. The last thing I need right now is for Andie to cry. When she cries, I cry, and I need to be tough right now. I'm barely holding it together, as is.

I force myself to smile as the car pulls up to the curb behind the Grand Arbor Hotel. Just before I get out of the car, I turn to Andie and tell her, "Nah, I won't be alone. Arthur said he's hiring some bodyguard to stay and watch over me while I'm stuck in the hotel."

"A bodyguard?" she asks, almost smiling again.

"Yep. Apparently the fact that I'm a strong, capable woman who works out, knows krav maga, and does her own stunts is not enough to keep me safe. *Apparently*, I need some rando dude to babysit me," I lament, rolling my eyes bitterly.

"Maybe Arthur is right about that," she begins, and before I can open my mouth to protest, she continues. "Just swallow your pride and let Arthur do his job, okay? I know you like to deal with shit on your own, but this is a serious situation. Your safety is the most important thing here. If that means you need to hire a whole barrel of big, muscular gym rats to stand guard while you sleep, then so be it. You know you're the most important person in the whole world to me, Molly, and I'll be damned if some slimy sleazeball like Eddie gets to hurt you. Besides, it's just temporary. Ride this out, and when it's over you can go back to being the tough, independent bitch you've been all along. Got it?"

I have to grin.

"Yeah, yeah. Message received. Humble pie devoured."

"Good," she says, smiling. "Love you, sis."

"Love you, too, Andie."

And with that, a security guard from the hotel comes out to help carry my stuff upstairs to my room. It's a massive, luxurious suite with a huge bed, a massive bathtub, and glossy, almost chrome furnishings. Well, if I have to be on lockdown, at least I get to be on lockdown in style.

I heave a sigh and plop down on the bed, staring up at the ceiling.

I just can't believe this is what my life has become. Holed up in some hotel by myself on Christmas Eve while my family gathers together like they do every year. I'm just lying here, helpless and vulnerable, waiting for my knight in shining armor to come protect me.

A *bodyguard.* I wrinkle my nose. Ugh.

A few minutes later, there's a sharp knock at the door, and it sounds frighteningly similar to the knocks on my apartment door that are almost always accompanied by a threatening letter from Eddie. I sit up and glance over at the door, my heart pounding.

The light coming in through under the door is punctured by shadows.

Someone is standing on the other side.

My logical brain tells me it's probably my stupid bodyguard. But that illogical, almost hysterical side of my brain insists that it's yet another one of those letters. One of Eddie's lowlife lackeys come to torture me. Or maybe, just maybe, it's Eddie himself.

I jump at the sound of a fist knocking at the door again.

Slowly, quietly, I get up and cross over the hardwood floor and try to look through the peephole. All I can see is black. Probably the stranger's shirt. With my hand shaking, I turn the knob and open the door.

My eyes widen and my mouth falls open in a gasp.

I never knew what *dumbstruck* really meant until this moment.

I'm face to face with the woman from the billboard. The woman I've been hired to protect. And in person, Molly Parker looks more stunning than anything I'd even thought about imagining. I never knew a photoshoot could dim someone's good looks, but this woman looks so good it's criminal.

Her hair spilling down her shoulder is like rich, dark wood, and it sets off the tone of her pale skin beautifully. Then there are those eyes that hold me paralyzed even though they just looked as stunned to see me as I am to see her.

Fuck me, I'm not starstruck, am I?

I always imagined getting glared at condescendingly by someone so famous, but Molly looks as stunned and frozen as I do. It almost feels like we're looking into mirrors, and before I know it, a full five seconds have passed with us just...taking each other in.

Then it wears off for us at about the same time, and she tries to slam the door in my face.

"Miss Parker," I nearly bark as I catch the door with one hand, keeping the heavy wood from getting thrust shut. Her face looks surprised and a little scared that I'm able to hold it open so easily. In the same moment, I take out my wallet and flash my security agent license in the crack of the door. "Wes Jameson. I'm the security you hired."

Her mouth hangs open for a moment as she seems too taken aback to talk. I knew she was famous for those lips, but standing in front of them, they're fuller than any camera could capture.

When she finally regains her senses, she gives her head a little shake, and color comes to her cheeks. "Security. Right. Um...come on in, sorry."

She pulls the door open and lets me step inside. I cast a glance behind me once more before I step in.

As the heavy door shuts behind me, the sound of the door shutting gives me plenty of information. Hollow steel frame filled with insulation to dampen sound. Solid-core, bonded wood. Automatic magnetic lock. The usuals you'd expect in a five-star hotel.

Next, I take in the room. With a name like the Grand Arbor, I was expecting luxury, but damn. The interior is wood-panel walls with chocolate brown trim and more wall-lights than I can count. It's roomy enough to be a big living room in a regular house, and there's a massive coffee table standing in the middle of it with a huge bouquet of flowers on it. A California king-size bed sits on a little raised platform of white tile above the rest of the light brown wooden flooring.

And in the middle of all of it is Molly Parker, running her fingers through her rich hair, standing there awkwardly. She's wearing jeans, a tank top, a cardigan, and her makeup isn't nearly as heavy as she has to keep it for camera appearances.

In the middle of all the luxury, I have to admit, she almost looks like a regular person.

"So uh...hi," she says with a nervous smile and a wave after tearing her eyes away from...was she checking me out? "Molly Parker. Sorry about that. Nice to meet you. Wes, you said?"

"Yep."

She nods, and there's another pause between us. Her cheeks go a little red. This is gonna be a long night.

"So," I say, breaking the tension and stepping into the room, slinging the heavy bag from off my back and setting it on the coffee table. "I'll be honest, the contract I got was a little slim on details, Miss Parker," I say as she backs away from me while I walk through the room. She's jumpy. That, and I stand out in this room like a bull in a china shop. "So I over prepared."

She comes a little closer to watch me take a large laptop and a few handfuls of wires out of my bag. I notice her eyes lingering on some of the ammunition I have in that bag, too. I have guns strapped to my torso, but she doesn't need to see those unless I need to use them.

"Anything you could possibly need for a one-person hotel room, I should have covered," I say simply, hooking up a few cords to the laptop and carry it over to the hotel phone, which I unplug, using the phone jack for one of my wires. I cast a glance around the room. "Can't guarantee this room was built for safety, though. You always lie low in... style?"

She looks a little indignant at that, but she tucks some hair behind her ear--probably an agitated habit--and brushes the comment off.

"It was short notice for me, too," she says. "Believe me, I wasn't planning to have to spend the holidays on my own either."

"Oh, so am I here to keep you company?" I ask with a mocking grin over my shoulder as I work. "I'll warn you, sweetheart, I'm no Santa, and this bag of surprises doesn't have any toys in it. Not the kind actresses like to play with, at least."

I catch a glimpse of her face screwing up into a scowl behind me.

"No, I was getting more of an 'abominable snow-man' vibe from that scruff you've got going on."

She's quick, I'll give her that.

"Really though, what are we looking at?"

She takes a breath and swallows, composing herself.

"Okay, so I don't know what you've heard in the news about me, but-"

"Nothing at all."

She blinks, staring at me blankly for a second.

"Wait, seriously?"

"Sorry, my life only started revolving around you about three minutes ago when I walked through that door, and it'll stop again when I walk back out."

She wrings her hands a little, pacing around the room behind me as she thinks a moment.

"Well excuse me, I didn't realize I was hiring a bodyguard who lives under a rock."

I'll admit, I had that one coming.

"I guess I should be happy about that. I wanted my lawyer to help keep everything under wraps, so I he must be doing a good job."

"You seem like you're a hard person to keep under wraps."

She ignores that.

"The short version is, you're here because I'm having trouble with my manager, and it's gotten serious."

I raise an eyebrow.

"Look, if you think I can intimidate someone into getting you a better contract…"

She sighs and shakes her head quickly.

"No no no, listen. Look, I know this is for work, but if I fill you in on everything, I need you to swear it won't get out to the public. I mean, I guess I don't exactly have another contract for that, but…"

I turn around and give her a flat stare, then glance down at my dusty leather jacket, jeans, boots, and rough hands. "Do I look like the kind of guy who gets out and talks?"

She gives me a weary look. "Outside of a saloon in a Clint Eastwood movie? No, not really."

I cross my arms and lean against the wall by the phone jack.

"Seriously though, I respect my clients' confidentiality. Nobody will even know I'm here working for you, if I have my way."

That seems to relax her a little, and she nods.

"Thank you. My manager, Eddie Arnold…" she pauses to compose herself. *Actresses.* "…is after me. Somehow. It all started a few weeks ago. I've known him since I was a little girl, but he made a pass at me that I was absolutely not comfortable with, and he didn't take the rejection well. But I had signed a contract that he'd gotten me to sign in a hurry, and in short, my career is…it's totally in his hands."

There's exasperation in her voice that I can't help but feel a twinge of sympathy for, and I frown. She's an actress, but I can tell when someone's holding genuine emotion back.

"So he's twisting the knife until you do something for him you don't want to do," I say, and she nods, swallowing.

"That's not even the half of it. Literally every piece of work that I could get goes through his desk. I don't even *know* about anything unless it goes through him. He owns me, and he's using that against me."

I'm starting to see where this is going. That kind of behavior strikes a chord with the kind of manipulative shit I saw in the mafia. And frankly, it makes me furious, even if it's a spoiled girl like Molly Parker getting jerked around.

"I thought that was going to be the worst of it," she goes on, "but then he threatened me. He said that if I don't come to him, he'll...he'll drag me back. Things got so intense so fast, and I found out my condo was compromised, so I moved here as quickly and quietly as I could. My parents don't even know I'm here."

"Slow down," I say, knitting my eyebrows. "Compromised how? Do you think he's going to try something drastic?"

"My lawyer thinks someone was heading to my condo," she says, nodding.

"Do you trust him?" I ask immediately, and her eyes go wide.

"My lawyer? Yes, he's one of the only people I *do* trust in all this. Believe me, if he was working for Eddie, he's had all the chances in the world to turn me over to him. He would have done it by now."

I nod in agreement, but there's a frown on my face. "Alright Miss Parker, kidnapping is a lot more serious than what the contract details led me to think. I really should have been briefed on more of this before coming into all this blind."

"Well, *you're* the one who took the job so quickly," she fires back, a little bite to her voice, and I raise my eyebrows. The next moment, she reins herself back in, breathing deeply. "I'm sorry, I shouldn't have snapped. I'm just...on edge after all this. And I'm not used to working with bodyguards, either."

"Really?" I say. "Here I thought little starlets didn't leave the house without a full entourage."

She shoots me a dirty look, and I raise my hands inoffensively and turn around to keep working on the phone jack.

"What are you doing, anyway?" she asks, moving closer to hover over me while I work. "I forgot your job is more than taking shots at my lifestyle."

"I'm tapping into the hotel's CCTV feed," I say gruffly, moving to the laptop to start checking my connection and setting up the stream. "If we're going to be bunkering up in a hotel room, I want to have eyes outside."

Her long eyelashes flutter in surprise.

"Oh. Is...is that legal?"

"I won't tell if you don't."

She doesn't find that as funny as I do.

I spend the next few minutes getting everything rigged up, including a little camera at the peephole in the door to give us a better, centralized feed for everything, and all the while, Molly is on my heels like a puppy, prodding me with questions about what's what. It's annoying, but I've dealt with worse.

By the time I finally get a visual on the CCTV security cameras and sit down, I hear a buzzing sound across the room.

"Oh--that's my phone," Molly says, moving to pick up her phone and answer it.

"You shouldn't be taking calls right now," I say without looking away from the screen.

"It's my lawyer," she says, "he's the only person I *can* talk to right now!"

I roll my eyes as she answers the phone.

"Hello?" I hear her say, and I keep my attention on the camera feed, but I can't help but hear her words. "Yeah, he's here getting set up and--what?" A pause. "You're kidding me," she says, her voice starting to shake a little. "Arthur, I'm backed into a hole here, I-"

I turn around, and I see her eyes rimmed with shining tears, a hand to her mouth.

"O-okay, but what do I-"

I snap my fingers at her, standing up and

approaching her. She nearly jumps, but puts her hand over the phone and asks "What?"

"Something I need to know?" I ask quickly.

"Eddie knows I'm here," she says, her voice thin and squeaking. It's the voice of someone truly backed into a corner. "Arthur says he has men on the way--we need to get out of here!"

"Give me the phone," I order, and she looks dumbstruck, but she's too shocked to protest when I take it from her hands.

I can hear a man's voice asking questions from the line, but I ignore it as I pry the phone open, to her horror. "What are you doing?!"

I see a little device under the phone's cover that confirms my suspicions, and I show it to Molly. "Your phone's bugged. That'll be how they tracked you."

Her face goes pale, and without another moment to spare, I put the phone on the ground and stomp my heel into it, shattering the thing.

Molly gasps, looking between me and it in shock. "Oh my god!"

"You need to be checking your phone for this kind of thing, if you're being chased," I say simply, keeping my voice calm.

"I just got that phone!" she exclaims.

I raise my eyebrow, and it dawns on her why that would explain the bug. She sits down on the couch, looking terrified.

"Oh my god, how many people does Eddie have coming after me?"

"If they had you bugged, they were likely tracking you," I say crossing back to my laptop and flipping through the channels on the security, and my heart starts to pick up at what I see.

This job just got a lot more interesting.

"What?" she asks, looking over at me, distressed.

"Your manager must have deep pockets," I say, my eyes focusing on some of the faces I see moving around the hotel. "And he must want you very badly."

"What are you talking about?" she snaps, hurrying over to my side, and I point to some of the men in each feed of the security.

"See these men here?" I point out a few of the people that have caught my attention in the cameras. "Bulky jackets, wide frames, look like they've seen combat? They aren't the types of people who stay in five-star hotels. I recognize them. They're 'security' who work for a company called North Sonoran Security. They're mercenaries, more or less. All veterans, all of their officers formerly involved in black ops. These are the kind of men drug lords hire."

It occurs to me that what I'm saying isn't exactly reassuring. I look over to see utter terror written on her face, and I add, "They don't know we can see them, though. But it does mean this is more serious than you could have known."

I expect her to break down, but instead, I watch her carefully compose herself, breathing deeply and stifling her fear to show a still, unreadable face. "Okay. Okay, there are military mercenaries here. For me. No problem."

Well, mostly composed.

I can't blame her, either. This is the big leagues.

"Stay calm," I say. "We know two things we didn't know a moment ago."

"What's that?"

"One: we know what lengths your friend Eddie is willing to go to, so he's going to have a hard time surprising us again," I say, my voice even. The next part is more complicated though, and my mind is already churning, going through the blueprints of the hotel I studied on the way over here, thinking about our options. I wasn't expecting to have to outwit special ops, but after all, the excitement is part of why I like this job.

"Two," I say, turning to look her in those sparkling amber eyes, "this hotel room is no longer safe."

MOLLY

Thump. Thump. Thump.

All I can hear is the pounding of my own heart, the blood rushing in my ears.

I turn away, almost in slow motion, like the world is grinding to a halt all around me, the background details fading into darkness and blurry shadows. I feel lightheaded, sick to my stomach, weak in the knees. All these feelings I'm not used to. Like I'm fragile. Like I'm weak.

This is not who I am.

This is not my life. It can't be.

I stumble my way across the room and into the en suite bathroom, closing the door behind me with a resounding click. I catch a glimpse of movement to my left and look up, terrified, just to see my own reflection staring wide-eyed back at me. It doesn't even look like me. I'm not accustomed to seeing my own face look so frightened. So pale and exhausted.

Suddenly, I'm filled with fury. This is not my fault. I didn't cause any of this to happen. I know that's what Eddie wants me to think. He wants me to blame myself. To regret how I responded to his disgusting advances. That's what he's banking on-- that I will give up and give in and come crawling back to him with my tail between my legs.

I can't help but wonder how many other women he's done this to. How many other girls have been cowed into submission? Convinced to give themselves over and relinquish their power to some fast-talking, manipulative asshole? Don't get me wrong, I'm no naive little ingenue like the media thinks I am. I'm not dumb. I'm no stranger to the ins and outs of the Hollywood game. I know there are predators out there just seething with opportunities to prey upon women young and old, drawing them in with promises of fame and stardom, only to dash their dreams to pieces and ruin their lives. Everyone here is desperate for one little shot at success, and all these guys have to do is dangle some fake connection or hookup on a string and girls come running. They throw caution to the wind and jump headlong into the deep end of the pool, not realizing that there are sharks in the water.

But me? I'm not like that. I'm shrewd. I'm careful. I grew up in this world and I watched my parents--

especially my mother-- navigating these tricky waters with expertise. I can usually spot a scam or a con artist from a mile away. I read between the lines. I examine the fine print.

Until Eddie came along and reassured me, made me think I was finally safe. He let me think I could relax a little bit, let him shoulder some of the burden of sifting through offers and scripts instead of going it alone. But it was all a trick. He just wanted me to lower my guard so he could slither through like the snake he is. And the worst part? It worked. He slid that contract in front of me like it was just routine business and I signed my whole soul away.

I grit my teeth, my hand gripping the edge of the bathroom counter as I try not to cry.

I should have seen this coming, somehow. I'm in control of my destiny. I always believed that so completely. I used to feel so strong. Now I just feel... violated.

Eddie's a sleazy guy who's been grooming me to be his little toy since I was a child. That much I'm already coming to terms with. But the idea that he could hate me so much that he would hire a bunch of mercenaries to come looking for me? That's crazy! That is the kind of thing that would happen in a movie I might star in, not my actual, real life.

I'm ripped out of my scary thoughts by the soft click of the bathroom doorknob turning. The door opens slowly and I turn to see Wes standing in the doorway, a serious look on his face.

"You done having a meltdown in here?" he asks. But even though his voice is gruff, I can detect what might just be a tiny note of sympathy. Gentleness, even.

But it disappears just as quickly as it appeared.

"We don't have all day," he says, "You saw those guys on the monitor. They're coming after you, whether you acknowledge it or not."

"I know that," I snap. "I'm fully aware of the situation, Mr. Jameson. I have been fucking living this situation for a couple weeks now. And I'm not having a 'meltdown,' I just needed a second to think without you looking at me."

A look of almost amusement crosses his face, and that makes me even angrier. He shakes his head. "Whatever you say, Miss Parker. Either way, we need to get a move on. Those men aren't going to wait until it's convenient for us. It's time to go."

"Go where?" I ask, frowning at him. "They're already *in* the hotel."

"Exactly," he says, turning and walking out of the bathroom without explaining himself any further. Where the hell did Arthur find this guy?! He is absolutely infuriating!

I have half a mind to just plant myself right here in this bathroom and refuse to move until he tells me the plan, but then I remember Andie's words to me. Reminding me to swallow my pride and just put up with whatever I have to in order to survive this situation. I roll my eyes up to the ceiling, take a deep breath, and walk out into the main living space of the hotel suite.

Mr. Jameson is bent over, digging through his bag of technology, tucking some smaller items into his jacket pockets. I peer over his shoulder ever so slightly and catch a flash of something metal and shiny. My heart skips a beat.

Is that... a fucking gun?

Before I can even ask, he turns back around and gives me an exaggerated once-over.

"What?" I ask, shrugging.

"Nothing. Just that you're not exactly dressed for the occasion," he says coolly.

"What occasion? Being hunted by mercenaries in the hotel where I was supposed to safely spend Christmas alone? Watching all my hard work evaporate in front of my face because of some nasty old man who wants what he can't have?" I exclaim, rather shrilly.

Again, he just gives me that semi-amused look. I wish I could slap that expression off his stupid, handsome face. What an insensitive asshole.

"No," he says, grabbing a fancy chair and dragging it over to the middle of the room. He climbs up onto the chair and begins fiddling with one of the ceiling tiles-- no, an air vent.

"Then what?" I press on, crossing my arms over my chest.

He looks down at me, setting the ceiling grate on the floor.

"An elaborate escape," he answers finally. And cryptically.

"Could you just, for once, give me a straight fucking answer," I mutter.

He steps down from the chair to stand right in front of me, towering over me with my nose almost pressed into his throat. I look up at him slowly.

"Fine," he says. "You're wearing what I can only assume are designer jeans, which, in their defense, do make your ass look fantastic, but are going to be pretty damn uncomfortable when you're climbing on your hands and knees."

I take a step back, my eyes going wide. "*Excuse* me?"

He smirks. "In the air vents. That's how we're going to get out of this room."

I look up at the ceiling, my heart skipping a beat.

"What?" I ask, incredulously. "What do you think this is-- a Bond movie?"

"No, of course not," he replies simply. "If it was a Bond movie, I'd be wearing a suit, and you'd be wearing way less clothing."

"You can't--"

"No time to argue. Are you coming with me or not?" he interjects, looking at me expectantly. I close my mouth and just stare at him for a moment, silently seething. Wherever Arthur found this guy, he's getting his ass chewed all the way out once all this is over.

"Feel free to hang out here until the mercenaries show up, if you'd rather do that."

"Fine. Fine! Whatever. Let's just go," I say, throwing up my hands in surrender.

"Great," he says, smiling roguishly. He offers me a hand and I push it away, walking around him to get up on the chair. He swivels around, saying, "Oh, come on, I know you're not going to be able to--"

His words fall short as I bend at the knees, jump up, and with my hands gripping the inside of the ceiling tiles, I carefully hoist myself up into the air vent. I look down through at the hole at him, just in time to see the look of shock and awe on his face before he swiftly wipes it away. Satisfying as hell.

"You coming or what?" I snap.

I can tell he's fighting a grin. "Well, back up a little so I have room," he says. And a moment later, he's swinging himself up into the cramped, dusty space with me. Suddenly we're face to face, only inches apart in the near-perfect darkness.

I swallow hard.

After a beat, he says quietly, "Follow me."

"How do you know where we're going?" I ask in the same muted tone.

He turns and starts crawling through the vent,

his perfect, taut ass a few feet in front of me. At least I'm going to have a nice view for this awful, doomed-to-fail plan of his.

He glances back over his shoulder. "I memorized the blueprint of the hotel."

"Uh-huh. Sure you did," I murmur.

"Do you really think I would put you-- or myself-- through this shit if I didn't know where I was going?" he retorts, his voice echoing ever so slightly in the metallic surroundings.

"Honestly? Maybe. I don't know you. Maybe this is fun for you," I say, admittedly a little more venomously than I planned.

"Oh trust me, sweetheart. I may have a wild idea of fun, but this sure as hell ain't it."

Thankfully, he can't see me rolling my eyes, and for the next several minutes or so, I just follow him dutifully in silence. I try not to focus too hard on how dumb an idea this is, how screwed we both are, how inevitable it is that the mercenaries-- if that is in fact what they are-- will find us. What will they do with me? Threaten me? Tie me up and intimidate me? Kidnap me and take me back to Eddie's office?

Kill me?

No. Nope. I can't think about that right now. So instead, I focus on the perfectly-sculpted ass in front of me, leading the way. As much of a dick as he is, I can't pretend for one single second that Mr. Wes

Jameson isn't ridiculously, annoyingly attractive. That scruffy face. Those crystalline-blue eyes.

And damn, that ass.

We keep moving, sometimes shimmying up through vertical piping, hosting ourselves onto the next level, until I have no earthly idea where the hell we are. We could be in another world by now, as far as I'm concerned. And as much as I don't want to admit it, the tight quarters are starting to make me nervous. Really nervous.

Nervous enough that I start breathing heavily. I can feel the panic settling in. I try to remind myself that even though it feels like I'm trapped, it's going to be okay. We're going to climb out the other end of these vents at some point and breathe freely again.

Suddenly, Mr. Jameson speaks again, softly. "Hey, you okay back there?"

"Uh, yeah. Yeah, of course," I answer quickly. Damn it, my voice is trembling.

He stops and looks back at me, genuinely concerned.

"Your breathing sounds different. You're not getting all panicky on me, are you?"

I shake my head vigorously, which only makes me feel dizzier. Oh shit.

He turns back to face me, but keeping a short distance away so as not to crowd me and make the claustrophobia even worse. There's a note of reassurance in his gruff voice. "I'm serious. Are you alright? We can slow down if you want."

"I'm fine. Really. It's just, uh, a little tight in here," I confess, my heart beating so loudly I'm afraid even he can hear it. He smiles, and it's such a genuine, true smile that it catches me off-guard. I didn't realize he was capable of such an emotion.

"I know. I hate this shit, too. Once when I was a kid, I thought it would be funny to hide in my mom's closet so I could jump out and scare her when she came home from work. Kids are such assholes. As luck would have it, as soon as I closed the closet door, a big box of old dishes fell in front of the closet. I couldn't get out. My mom worked late that night, so I was stuck in there for probably four or five hours. By the time she came home and found me, I was a wreck," he says, laughing gently.

"God, that sounds horrible," I tell him honestly

He shrugs. "Yeah. It sucked. But now whenever I'm in a tight space like this, I remind myself that if I could survive being trapped in a closet for hours as a kid, then I sure as hell can handle it now as an adult."

Against my better judgment, I smile. "Makes sense."

To my surprise, I've totally stopped hyperventilating. My head is clear. It worked.

"I feel better now. Sorry to slow us down," I tell him. He shrugs and turns back around to keep leading us through the vents.

"No big deal. Sometimes you have to stop and breathe. Besides, if I'm being honest, it's pretty fucking impressive that you were able to swing yourself up into the vents in the first place. That takes a lot of strength that I… did not expect you to have," he confesses.

"It's okay. Nobody ever expects shit like that from me. I know what I look like, you know. People underestimate me all the time," I tell him, still surprised at how civil our conversation has become.

"Where the hell did you learn how to do that, anyway?" he asks.

"Acting," I answer shortly. He snorts. "No, really," I add. "I do my own stunts. It's part of my job description to be in shape, to be able to handle myself."

"Well, I'll be damned," Mr. Jameson says, and there's real appreciation in his tone.

We continue on for awhile longer, and I have no idea how much time has passed. My eyes have adjusted to the darkness, only punctured by the little flashlight in Mr. Jameson's hand. I would never, ever admit it, but my hands and knees are starting to ache from crawling along like this. I'm definitely going to have bruises. But I try to keep my mind free. I can't dwell on the bad stuff. Not right now. I try to release all those worries and anxieties, clear my head like I do before I film a particularly emotional or physical scene at work. Andie taught me meditation a couple years ago, when she was first getting into the whole yoga thing. I can't say it's my favorite thing to do. I've got too much on my mind to be constantly erasing it all in the pursuit of some impossible calm. But sometimes it's useful. Like now.

In fact, I clear my mind so effectively that I almost jump out of my skin when Mr. Jameson speaks up again, stopping short in front of me.

"This is it. This is the top," he says. "This is where we get out."

"Where are we?" I ask.

"I just said: the top. We're going to the roof."

"Seems like a weird place to try and hide--"

"Just trust me, okay?" he says, giving me an impatient look.

"Alright. Jeez. Calm down," I mumble.

He takes a few moments to dislodge the grate in front of us, then he carefully lifts it up into the shaft before peering down into a hallway identical to the one outside my hotel suite. Quietly and cautiously, he lowers himself down. He offers me a hand, and I swallow my pride for the hundredth time, taking it.

When my feet touch the ground, I take a deep breath of relief, happy to be out of that tiny, claustrophobic vent shaft. Wordlessly, he gestures for me to follow him down the hall to a small staircase with a door at the top. We walk up the steps, our footsteps soft enough to barely make any noise at all, and he punches a code into the door, then opens it.

We step out onto the roof, the brisk December air hitting me and making goosebumps pop up on my skin instantly. Shivering slightly, I follow Mr. Jameson across the roof while the sun sets radiantly over the city of Los Angeles. The sky is streaked with pink and gold, the air just cold enough to remind me that this is Christmas.

"Okay. So, from here, we're going to the safe room access point," Mr. Jameson explains, leading me around to the other side of a gigantic concrete water tank. "The safe room has everything we'll need for the night. Once we're there, we'll be--"

His words are cut off as he suddenly stops walking. A few steps behind him, I nearly bump into him before I realize why we're standing still. Three men are surrounding us, guns pointed at us.

"--safe," Mr. Jameson finishes, barely audible in the calm before the storm.

Reflexes kick in.

Faster than a breath, my body moves in front of Molly, standing as broadly as I can while my hand whips my gun out, and within a second, I've fired three rounds in front of me. There's no thought involved, no time to plan. Just pure instinct.

I don't think even Molly had time to register what was happening.

Working security goes against everything biology tells the human body to do. When a gun is pointed at you and you're staring down a barrel that can end your life, instinct and basic strategy tells you to make yourself as small a target as possible, to shrink away.

A bodyguard has to do the opposite.

The fact that the three men ahead of us are taken

by almost as much surprise as we are is what saves my life.

Each one of my bullets hits true. The first man takes the shot to the crook of his elbow, and he cries out in pain as his weapon falls to the ground. The second man gets hit in the shoulder, and when he shoots back at me, it's a wild miss. The next second, he grabs his injured friend, and the two of them struggle to cover behind an air unit.

The third man gets hit in the leg, but while his two comrades move right, he starts to move backward, keeping his gun level.

He would have gotten a shot off at me, if the unexpected hadn't happened.

Molly slips out from behind me.

"No!" I shout.

Immediately, I reach out to grab her back, but she moves too fast for me to grab, closing the short distance between me and the mercenaries in an instant. And in that moment, I see the logic in what she's doing.

The mercenary turns his gun up, away from Molly's person. They must be under strict instructions not to harm her, much less shoot her.

He takes one hand off his gun, preparing to grab her and wrestle her, but he's as surprised as I am when her hands flash forward, clapping around the wrist of the gunman and twisting. He cries out in pain as the gun clatters to the ground, and she kicks it far away from them as she twists his arm around his back.

My mind flashes back to the sight of Molly climbing up into the vents like she was born doing it. This little brat is full of surprises.

I don't have any time to watch her, though, because the men behind the air unit will be finding their courage again in a few moments.

Wasting no time, I dart for the unit, knowing that right now, keeping up the element of surprise and staying on the offensive is what will win this fight for us.

These mercenaries came here expecting to have to capture a scared, defenseless girl. We have to use that to our advantage.

Caution to the wind, I haul myself up on top of the air unit and come at them from above. I leap over to see two stunned, masked faces below me, each ready to fire around the side of the unit.

Immediately, I descend on the one I shot in the shoulder, diving head first into him. There's a bang, and I hear my ears ringing--his gun must have gone off next to my head, but I don't feel pain, so I keep at him. His body slams back down into the concrete, and I grapple with him.

His reflexes are better than I thought, and it's not easy to get behind him, but his injury makes it hard for him to resist as I turn him around.

Next to me, the other man with the elbow injury

tries to kick my head in, but I put the shoulder-guy in a headlock with one arm while I grab the other man by the ankle, stopping his kick. With a solid twist, I bring him to his knees with a howl of pain.

Still holding onto the one man's head, I stand up with the second one's leg in my other hand. With a swift motion, I lift my foot and bring it crashing into his knee. There's a sickening crack and a scream of pain as his knee caves in. That's the end of his mercenary career.

While he writhes on the ground, I turn my attention back to the man I have in a headlock, who's trying to elbow me in the kidney. With a grunt, I haul him up, facing the air unit, and I bring his forehead crashing into the cold metal.

With a loud clang of skull against metal, he goes limp, knocked out cold.

As his body slumps down, I seize the gun from his hands, turning around to the man with the injured leg. I grab him by the collar, and he opens his eyes in time to see me bringing the butt of the handgun down onto his forehead, pistol-whipping him into unconsciousness as well.

I don't need bodies on my hands tonight.

Both my gun and his in hand, I swiftly move to help Molly with her fight, but when I round the corner of the unit, I see her with a high-heel planted firmly on the man's chest, and she's pointing a pistol at him. His hands are up, and he looks terrified.

I have to admit, it does look like something right out of a movie.

"Good job," I grunt as I move toward them, putting one gun away and holding the other in position to put the third guy's daylights out like the other two. "Let's get him knocked out and get out of here."

"Hold on," Molly says, glaring down at her prisoner. I arch an eyebrow.

"What? I mean, we *can* kill him, but it's a lot messier than the movies make you think-"

"I want to let this one go," she says, and both me and the mercenary look surprised.

"Seriously?" he says.

"Shut up," both me and Molly say at the same time, then glance at each other.

"I want one of these fucks to go back to Eddie with his tail between his legs," she says, and even I'm surprised by the fire in her eyes. It...suits her, I'm surprised to find myself thinking. "If he wants a war, he'll get one."

There's a pause from all of us, and Molly breaks it by aiming her gun further south, between the mercenary's legs, and I can see him seizing up. "Got that, jackass?"

"Yes m'am!" he barks back.

"Good," I say coming forward and gesturing with my gun. "Now get on your feet, hands where I can see them.

He obeys, and I pat the man down, disarming

him of his side-weapons and a knife, including his wallet and phone. Once he's totally clean, I step back, and Molly lowers her gun.

"Go," I bark, "straight down and out of here, don't talk to anyone."

He nods, and as soon as he has our permission, he darts for the nearest door and heads downstairs.

The moment he's out of sight, I look to Molly, and almost at the same second, her hardened expression melts away to the shaken, terrified one I was expecting.

"Oh my fucking god they had guns," she breathes, letting a sob out of her chest as she tries to keep a hold of herself. "They had fucking guns--they almost shot you!"

"You handled yourself...surprisingly well a second ago," I say, eyebrows raised.

"It's called acting, ass-hat," she says as she sniffs. "I literally do it for a living."

I nod. "Huh. Fair enough. That move with his wrist sure as hell wasn't acting, though."

"Self-defense classes," she explains, rolling her shoulders back and handing me the gun, suddenly uncomfortable holding it. "I mean, I took that for myself, but it helps with acting, too. I do my own stunts, remember? And I want it to look real when I do, y'know, stuff like that."

She looks over at the two unconscious men by the air unit. "Not that I ever expected to have to use it on actual kidnappers with actual military training. Jesus."

"Life imitates art, I guess," I say with a chuckle, and that earns a sincere smile from her.

Maybe it's the adrenaline pulsing through my veins, but the sight of those lips of hers smiling makes my heart pick up. I feel movement between my legs, watching her chest rise and fall with her quick breathing, eyes still lit up from the action. *Shit, get a hold of yourself, Wes.*

But when I get a hold of myself and tear my eyes away, I realize she was giving me the same look, and I catch a hint of red in her cheeks before my eyes fall on the unconscious men.

"So what do we do with them?" she says suddenly after clearing her throat.

"Give me a hand," I say, and together, we drag the two of them to the metal ladder and a pipe running up the side of the water tank. I tear off some of their clothes and use that to tie them to it with practiced ease. Back to business, my reflexes make my demeanor cold and calculating once again, and I move with machine-like efficiency.

Within a couple of minutes, their hands and feet are bound, and their mouths are gagged.

"When these two wake up," I say, tightening their bindings, "they'll be useful as hostages. NSS is a mercenary company, but they take care of their own. The fact that we've got these two guys in our hands is the only thing keeping that coward we spared from ratting on us and having the rest of the kidnappers running up here to take us down."

"Oh shit, I didn't even think about that!" Molly gasps, suddenly looking terrified, but I put a hand out.

"That's why we keep these guys here. If your little messenger doesn't talk, then these two might be here long enough to wake up and give us some information while they're still useful to us."

There's a cold edge to my voice, and I feel Molly's gaze on me. I look over at her, and she gives her head a little shake.

"Sorry. I just didn't realize bodyguards could be so...um..."

"Ruthless?" I finish with a lopsided smile. "Sure, I'm a regular Al Pacino. Look, I'm just keeping our bases covered. And I'm not half as bad as these mercenaries can get."

What I don't tell her is that the whole reason I know about NSS is their connection to some of the most dangerous mafia leaders in the Southwest.

"Sure," she says, nodding, then she takes a breath and puts her hands on her hips. "So, what now?"

I frown. "We wait. Eddie might be desperate, but judging by how these mercenaries are acting, he doesn't want this to become a public battle any more than you do. If the mercenaries stick around the hotel too long, they'll tip someone off that they're suspicious, and then it's only a matter of time before police get called."

She nods, following my logic. "Okay, but...where do we wait them out? You said the hotel room's not safe. Do we just stay on the roof all night?"

"Even if I really wanted to put you through hell, I wouldn't do that," I say with a laugh, but she doesn't seem to find the idea as funny. "No, that's putting too much faith in the guy heading downstairs. There might be more people coming up after him. We can't stay here. There's only one place in the hotel we can ride out the night."

"What's that?"

I point to a utility elevator across the roof. "That's part of why I brought us up here. That's an access shaft that leads right down the spine of the hotel. It'll lead us right where I want to take us, but you're not going to like it."

I start to walk toward the door I pointed to, and I hear her heels clicking after me as she asks, "What do you mean though?"

I glance back at her. "We're spending the night in the safe room. Together."

I'm getting really, really tired of following this guy around.

Don't get me wrong, he's an attractive figure to look at from behind, but it seems like the last several hours have been nothing but Mr. Jameson leading me through some labyrinth where no matter where we go, we end having to move on to somewhere worse. As if crawling through the air vents like a pair of raccoons wasn't bad enough, we now have an official rooftop battle under our belts. I'm starting to wonder if I'm actually just on some awful celebrity prank show or something. All of this feels so separate, so alien compared to my usual daily life. I just want so badly to go back to what I know, the world I'm comfortable in. Where I know just who I am and where I stand. But that's behind me now. Eddie took that away from me.

And now? Instead of spending Christmas with my family, relaxing and looking forward to some much-needed time off, I'm in a narrow elevator with a strange man who is turning out to be way more than I bargained for when Arthur suggested hiring a bodyguard. This guy, this Wes Jameson, is less bouncer and more... I don't know. International man of mystery? Gangster?

Killer?

I gulp. The way he manhandled those goons up on the roof really puts me on edge. That wasn't just some inexperienced scuffle. He wasn't lucky to escape with his life-- *they* were. He took charge like it was his purest instinct, like all he had to do was zone out and go into attack mode. I know what a real fight looks like. At the boxing studio where I take my classes, I've been witness to more than one fight that got out of hand. Maybe one guy makes a remark about his opponent's mother or girlfriend. Pushes him too far. And the next thing you know, there's blood splattering the floor and whistles blowing shrilly in the air. Of course, it's never happened to me before. I keep to myself. I'm quiet and observant, watching and learning rather than trying to play it off like I'm cocky. Sure, I could have signed up for classes at a less violent, more above-ground location. Taken some lessons with a woman who's more concerned with sculpting my glutes than teaching me how to truly disarm an attacker. In other words, I could have taken the kind of class people expect me to take.

But that's not what I wanted. I'm dedicated to my craft, to making every scene look and feel as real and authentic as possible. So yeah, I go to the seedy part of town for my boxing lessons. That's why I know what real danger looks like.

And Wes Jameson? He's real danger. That much I can tell already.

The elevator dings and the little light flashes above the metal doors as they split open. He looks back at me, nodding for me to follow him out into a small, tight entryway. He types a code into the door in front of us and it clinks open, whining a little as though it hasn't been opened in a long time. And honestly, it probably hasn't. How often does a hotel safe room really need to e opened up in Los Angeles?

"This is it," Mr. Jameson says. "Home sweet home for the night."

I walk around him into the room. It's not as awful as I assumed. I was expecting an eight-by-eight-foot concrete cell or something. This just looks like a relatively spartan hotel room, with a twin bed pushed against a wall in the corner, stark white sheets and a single fluffy pillow dressing it. The floor is hardwood, to my surprise, instead of poured concrete. The walls are a nondescript gray, a simple circline ceiling lamp illuminating the room. Every minute or so, it flickers slightly, which does add just a hint of derelict abandon to the space. To my relief, there is a tiny en-suite bathroom with a standing shower and a miniature sink basin. Against the opposite wall is possibly the world's tiniest kitchenette. A little sink, mini-fridge the size of a small microwave, and a single stovetop unit flanked by cabinets which, I'm sure, are filled with cups, plates, and cooking utensils.

"Not five-star by any means," Mr. Jameson says, standing directly behind me. His breath hot on the back of my head makes me shiver. "But it could be much worse."

I turn and give him a weak smile. "Yeah. It's kind of cute, actually."

He raises an eyebrow. "Cute? I think this may be the first time in human history that a utilitarian safe room has ever been described as 'cute.'"

I shrug and walk over to the bed, sitting down on the edge. It crinkles and groans at my weight, like it's been untouched for months except for when the sheets get washed.

"Reminds me of my first apartment when I moved out of my parents' house at eighteen," I explain, looking around the blank room. "It was a studio. Teeny-tiny. I could've gotten a roommate or just taken my parents up on their offer to get me a nicer place. Hell, when I landed that movie, the producer offered me a place at one of the properties he owned. A huge house. Five bedrooms, four baths.

Way too much for one person. But I was so excited to finally pay for my own place, and I wanted to do it the old-fashioned way. Scrimp and save."

I smile at the memory. I can still remember how excited I was, the butterflies in my stomach when that grouchy landlord handed me the key to my first studio apartment.

"That's crazy," Mr. Jameson says, looking at me quizzically. "Why would you live in a cardboard box if you could afford something so much nicer?"

I think about it for a second, trying to figure out how to word my answer.

"Well," I begin, sighing, "when you grow up surrounded by money and opulence and fancy stuff, it gets a little old. Don't get me wrong-- I'm so grateful for my upbringing. I never wanted for anything. My parents didn't spoil us, exactly, but we got what we needed and more. I remember when I was a teen, I would watch these movies about people trying to make it in the big city, living in their mouse-infested little apartments, just working hard to get by. I remember thinking, 'Wow, that's so cool. That is what I want.' So as soon as I got the chance, that's exactly what I did. I never want to take my money, my privilege, for granted. Besides, in my job, I'm not planning to try out for the role of Rich Bitch or Spoiled Primadonna. I already lived that life. If I'm going to make a living out of pretending to be someone I'm not, then I want to, you know, go for the roles that are different from how my real life is. And to really capture what it's like to live like a normal, non-famous person, I need some experience living that way. In reality. If that even makes any sense at all," I finish, blushing as I realize I've been rambling.

Mr. Jameson is looking at me with a funny look on his face, the corners of his mouth starting to tug upward into a hint of a smile, but his eyes-- those gorgeous blue eyes-- look so serious. So contemplative. Like he's reassessing everything he thought about me to begin with.

"What?" I ask, cocking my head to one side.

He shakes his head, that smile warming his handsome features. He swipes a hand over his scruffy jawline. "Nothing. You're just... different. From what I expected."

"In a good way or a bad way?" I ask, and immediately regret the question. I know how it makes me sound. Eager. Insecure. Self-centered.

He laughs softly, backing up to lean against the wall with his muscular arms crossed over that broad, powerful chest. "Neither. Hmm. A good way, I guess."

"Oh," I answer lamely, quickly looking down at the hardwood floor. What's the matter with me all of a sudden? Why am I blushing and averting my eyes like some flustered school girl? I'm a grown-ass woman in a very serious situation, and here I am acting like a teenager.

Get a grip, Molly Parker, I tell myself. I need to change the subject. This tiny, silent room is beginning to feel a little cramped, even though we are at opposite ends of the room.

"You're not exactly what I expected, either," I tell him, breaking the quiet.

He looks up at me, eyes blazing. My heart pounds.

"How so?" he asks, his voice low and gruff.

"I don't know. I've never had a bodyguard before, but I mean, I've watched a lot of movies. And you-- you're not what I thought you'd be. That's all," I conclude, shrugging. God, I wish I hadn't said anything. I thought it was an innocent enough comment, but he looks as though I've touched on a raw nerve somehow.

"Shouldn't judge a book by its cover, you know," he replies simply. I can tell he's trying to regain his former demeanor, that cocky attitude he had before. But it's slipped away.

"I'm sorry, Mr. Jameson. I know you probably don't want to be stuck here with me over Christmas," I blurt out suddenly. "I'm sure you have a family or-- a wife or someone you would much rather be with right now. And I just wanted to say I'm sorry. And thank you. For looking after me. I know it's not ideal."

"Wes."

"What?" I ask, frowning.

He fixes me with that intense stare. It's like he can see directly into the core of my being, the corners of my soul where nobody dares to look. "My name is Wes. You can just call me that."

"Oh. Well, in that case, you can call me Molly," I reply, smiling.

"Molly Parker. You know, your face is right outside my office window," he remarks suddenly. "Big-ass billboard for some shampoo or whatever."

I can feel my cheeks burning. "Oh god. That's super embarrassing."

"Nah. It's your job. Just like this is my job. We all do what we have to do to get by. And sometimes, people look at you and think they can know who and what you are with just that one quick glance. Like your job, your image-- that's all you are. I guess for some people, maybe that's true. But I don't think it is for you," he says slowly.

Something about the way he's looking at me makes me tremble.

"So, what do you think, then? About me," I inquire softly.

"Well, at first, I would have judged you by that billboard. By those designer jeans. By your famous last name. But that's not enough. That's not really you, is it?"

I shake my head. "I hope not."

"No. You're more than I expected. You're tough. You fight. You have no problem getting your hands dirty. You're smarter than you look. You're feisty. And you're strong. And I think you listen a lot more than you speak. You notice things," Wes says. "I can see it, those cogs turning in your mind. I can feel you analyzing, constantly. Trying to figure shit out."

"Wow," I murmur, looking down at the floor.

"What is it?" he asks, walking over to me slowly.

I look up back up at him as he stops in front of me. A smile creeps to my lips. "Nothing. It's just-- that may be the best review I've ever gotten."

Wes sits next to me on the bed. I can feel the warmth radiating off of his body. It makes my heart race. Makes my stomach feel all wobbly in the very best way.

Oh yes. Wes Jameson is danger, all right. And you'd think I'd already have reached my limit with danger, but…

Suddenly he stands up, like the heat between us has finally burned him. He holds out a hand to me. I look at it confusedly at first. "Come on. We have a whole night to kill, and I know you're not sleepy. Show me your moves."

"What? Dancing?" I ask, wrinkling my nose at him. He chuckles.

"No, sweetheart. Fighting. Boxing. I wanna know how you learned to handle yourself in a fight the way you did up on the roof. Maybe you can even teach *me* something," he adds, a sliver of that familiar arrogance slipping through as he grins.

After a moment of hesitation, I take his hand and stand up. I kick off my heels so that I'm barefoot. He leaps back and puts up his fists, nodding for me to come at him. I can't help but laugh, a genuine smile crossing my face as I square up. "Alright, Rocky, let's see how you fare against me," I egg him on.

"Ladies first," Wes remarks, smirking.

I pull a fake-out, like I'm rearing back for a right hook, but instead I duck down and pounce at his stomach, hooking one of my legs around his and nearly bringing him to the ground. He laughs and stumbles for a moment before regaining his balance. I dart backward out of the way as he lunges for me, then swivel around and leap at his back. I catch him with an arm around his throat, careful not to actually choke him at all. He reaches back to grab me, but I've got my legs tight around his waist. So he swings forward, throwing me off. Luckily, I saw this coming, and I land with a little bounce on my bare feet before turning back. With a fire flashing in his eyes, he comes running at me, and to my disappointment, I'm so entranced by his stare that my reflexes are just ever-so-slightly slowed down. My mind going blank, I simply back up, sliding into the wall as Wes bolts forward and pins me there, his arms on either side of me against the wall. He's less than an inch away, the two of us panting, eyes locked together.

I can feel that blaze between us, pulsing like a third heartbeat.

My eyes flick down, dangerously, to linger on his lips.

Slowly, he moves closer, and I don't dare to stop him. I can't. I don't want him to stop.

He kisses me, sending spirals of sparks down through my core, electrifying every nerve in my body. He presses up against me so I can feel every rippling muscle in his form. His cock is hard against my stomach, his hands coming down to cup my face as his tongue pushes inside my mouth. I moan into the kiss, melting under his touch. He hoists me up, my legs wrapping tightly around his waist as he rocks against me. I tangle my fingers in his scruffy hair, never wanting to break away from this moment. God, it's been years since I felt like this. My career has consumed every bit of free time, closed my heart and body off to even the idea of dating, of sex.

And now… this gorgeous, powerful man is holding me in his arms, kissing me like I've never been kissed before. I want him. So badly. No, I need him.

He breaks away and looks at me, his eyes deep blue and questioning.

This is a bad idea. This is a *terrible* idea. The worst idea of all time.

Or is it? What the hell else are we going to do locked up here in this tiny room while my life spins apart into shambles outside? I don't want to think about that. I don't want to think at all. And I have a feeling Wes knows just how to make me forget my troubles, at least for a little while. His lips brush against mine faintly, asking a silent question.

Should we?

I've done terrible things in my life. I've threatened people, I've stolen money, and I've done the bidding of the mafia.

This is still the worst mistake I've ever made. And it feels sweeter than all the rest combined.

I press a kiss into her again.

The warmth of her lips on mine awakens something in me I never thought I was able to feel, much less feel for someone like Molly Parker--for this spoiled actress of all people--she's a client, for god's sake.

It was a mistake I knew I was going to make from the moment she wrapped those endlessly long legs around my waist, and I felt her thighs squeezing me, her hips pushing up into me, those eyes drinking me in...it was all over.

The kiss is fierce. The adrenaline of the fight is

still red-hot in our blood, pulsing through my veins. It beats in my heart, and I can feel hers beating against me as I pull her in, hold her tight, and feel her chest rub up against mine. She's famous for her lips, and now, I can see why.

But nobody else has *touched* them like this, felt them pressing against mine, feeling my rough, scruffy face on her skin, skin that's been pampered this woman's entire life.

Every part of her is infuriating. She's everything I've been bitter about my entire life. And now, I can't keep my hands off her.

I feel her tongue venture out and touch mine, meeting it at our teeth before mine enters her mouth, where she welcomes me. As I move my jaw, my teeth toy with her lips, pulling away ever so slightly before coming back in again.

Her nails dig into my back, and she pushes her hips into me harder. She starts thrusting ever so slightly, almost unconsciously, her body moving out of pure need. It's undignified. It's animalistic. And I'm feeding every moment of it, fanning those flames hotter.

I grind my hips against hers, feeling my manhood growing harder and thicker. It's pressed up against her lower lips, and there's so much warmth between us that I want the fabric separating us to just burn away with the friction. With every thrust, my cock gets harder, and the bigger it swells, the more excited I can feel my little client getting in my grasp. Her fingers fumble as they try to keep hold of me. I feel her draw in a sharp breath.

This poor woman has no idea what she's getting herself into.

It doesn't matter if she's an untouched virgin or if she thinks she has some experience. I can tell by the way she moves nervously through her lust that she is in no way ready for what I have to give her.

Finally our kiss breaks, and we look at each other, breathing heavily, both our eyes laden with need. I raise my hand and cup her head in it, gently sliding my fingers in her soft hair, holding her head, watching her blushing face.

There's only one question on my lips.

"Do you want this?"

I expect her to be hesitant, to think about her career and what this could mean in the middle of a scandal, even to fire me on the spot and regret everything about the last twenty-four hours.

Instead, she nods without a second thought, those amber eyes holding me spellbound. "I want you in me, Wes."

I don't need a second invitation.

My mouth goes to her neck, kissing up and down the sensitive skin of this woman worth millions of dollars. With my hips pinning her to the wall, I bring my arms to her chest and grope her breasts. My huge hands cover them entirely, feeling them through her shirt, and with every second, I get hungrier for more.

One of my hands slides around to her back, my tough hands gliding along that unbelievably expensive fabric while my teeth graze her neck. I get a hold of her ass and pinch her, making her jerk up into me with a gasp.

Her ass is impeccably firm. It's unlike any I've ever felt before.

The next moment, I realize her hands are exploring me, too, and I let her warm hands take in as much as they want. They start at my waist, just above where her thighs are holding onto me, not doing so much as twitching despite the incredible effort it must take for her to hold on like this for so long.

I'm rock-hard down there, like the rest of my body. Her fingertips run up and down my abs, occasionally curling in and scratching me, wanting to dig in even harder. I push myself further in to invite her to do just that.

In response, she slips her fingers under my shirt and starts to feel my bare skin. I'm jealous, wanting to bring my mouth to her bare breasts, but I'm patient. My chest swells and falls with each breath while I feast on her neck, and she manages to nearly work her hands to my bare chest, feeling my hair, there, taking a handful of it and silently begging me for more.

Before I know it, even with her legs off the ground, she's managed to get my shirt halfway off, and I grin into her neck before I move my hands to her wrists and pin her against the wall, touching my forehead to hers.

"You're getting greedy, you little brat."

"I always get what I want," she teases back, and I feel my cock pulse against her. She bites her lip through a smile. She enjoys getting this kind of stir out of me.

And damn her, there's nothing I can do to deny her.

She scoots herself up the wall as I release her arms, and she rests them on my shoulders for a moment before I rip my shirt off and toss it to the floor.

Her hands help hold her up behind my thick, rippling neck. Her lidded eyes look me up and down, from the point where are crotches are kissing together to the wall of my solid abs to my broad, hairy chest, glistening from the heat between us as it breathes slowly.

The look on her face makes me want her all the more. She looks hungry, but her caution just says that she wants to savor it.

"I've done scenes like this before," she breathes, her voice low and smooth as silk, "just between actors, but it's all faked. His hands are usually cold, and they've got this sleeve-thing for his dick so I can't feel it if he gets excited."

"I don't think I have to tell you how much they need it," I growl back at her, and she giggles, turning her head away, but I take her by the chin and bring her face close to mine, running my thumb along the line of her jaw.

Without breaking eye contact, I move a hand to her tanktop and feel the fabric between a thumb and forefinger.

"I want this off."

"Then why don't you try to take it?" she challenges me.

I'm going to like this girl.

I pull us back from the wall and spin around to the bed, tossing her down on it like a ragdoll, watching her bounce on her back with a wicked laugh coming from her lips that drives me wild for her. I kick off my shoes and approach her, looming over her looking as savage as she does beautiful.

She writhes on simple sheets, looking up to me with anticipation, her cheeks going redder than ever. Her eyes look me up and down, getting her first look at my whole body standing over her. She lets her gaze rest on the outline of the thick shaft bulging through my jeans.

As she squirms, I grab her thighs and pull her closer to me, working my hands up to the waist of her pants and sliding my fingers around to the front.

Along the way, I feel the soft fabric of her underwear beneath it.

"You must be wearing more than I make in a month," I say.

"One way to find out," she breathes.

I unbutton her pants and pull them down to reveal the most intricate lace panties I've ever seen. They look like a work of art--top of the line, designer underwear. She wasn't even dressing for lingerie. Is this really her everyday wardrobe?

She twists her body to help get herself out of the pants, and without missing a beat, I go for the top next. I spend less time with it. I pull the fabric off and toss it aside, leaving her with nothing but underwear and me in nothing but my jeans.

I crawl on top of her, and the sight of her below me, watching my every movement with lustful antic-ipation, makes me want to thrust myself into her right now. But I'm going to take my time with her.

It isn't everyday you get a Hollywood starlet wrapped around your cock.

I descend on her and draw her into a kiss, feeling her soft moan up into me while my hands slip behind her back and unhook her bra. It comes off effortlessly for me, and I don't break our kiss while I slide it from her arms.

When the kiss finally ends, I look down at her and see her naked form, and the animal within me wants to ravage her.

I always hated the way actresses like her look up on the screen or advertisements. The camera does such unnatural things to the human body that it's hard to see the people behind all the glamour.

But when I look down at Molly, I realize the camera is doing a disservice to her. The real woman is far more beautiful than the best camera work could make her look.

My hands take her bare breasts and stroke them gently, fingers tracing along their sides while my thumbs feel her nipples.

The simple motion makes her gasp, and she arches her back up into me, pouting lips open and breathing desperately.

I start moving my thumbs in a circle around her stiff nipples, toying with them like I have all the time in the world to use her body any way I want. But I can't keep my hunger in check for too long.

My grip on her breasts gets more greedy. As I feel her up, she reaches up with both hands, one going to my face to feel my hair and my beard, the other going to my cock, her thumb stroking up and down its length and making it twitch under her hand.

Feeling her soft touch on my face is not something I'm used to. It would be soothing, if I weren't a few seconds away from diving into her. Every move her body makes warms my body and gives me a thrill that I must work out on her.

"I want to see it," she says, her eyes looking down

at my cock, then flitting back up to me. "I want to touch it."

"We're making a big mistake, Miss Parker," my husky voice whispers to her.

"Then let's make it before we come to our senses," she begs me, her eyes dancing with fire.

I stand up and unbutton my pants, and from the moment I start to slide them down, her eyes are on me, her body propped up on her elbows. I'm used to her eyes always looking a little mysterious, lidded, watching carefully. When the base of my shaft is exposed, all of that melts away, and her eyes go so wide I can see their whites.

"Oh my god," she says, the almost theatrical lust giving way to genuine surprise at the sight of my cock.

I pull my pants off and let them fall to the ground, giving her a lopsided smile as I put a knee on the bed and move toward her. She's frozen, her mouth hanging open at the sight of my manhood half-erect before her.

"Still sure, or are you having second thoughts, sweetheart?"

She swallows, but she looks up into my eyes, resolute. "I wanna know what you can do to me."

I practically lunge forward, and she falls on her back, legs spread before me, the challenge in her voice spurring me on. This little brat really does know how to get what she wants. I wonder if she knows just what she's getting into.

My hands go to her panties, and I pull them up, bringing her legs together and lifting them up as I pull the fabric off. Rather than letting her legs fall back down, though, I catch her by the ankles once the fabric is fluttering to the bed by the side.

Her face looks scared and excited all at once, and her fingers are sliding to her exposed slit. The moment they make contact, I can hear just how ready she is and see the glimmer of her honey shining on her fingers.

"Impatient, aren't you?" I chuckle as I rest her ankles on my shoulders, looking down her bare legs to her needy form. Her free hand is toying with her nipple like I was a moment ago. Her lips curl up in a smile that I'm about to wipe from her face.

I put my hands on her thighs, then put the tip of my stiff cock on her lips, letting my crown meet the tip of her finger.

She draws it back as if touched by fire, and she gasps, looking down at it. For a moment, there's reluctance on her face, as if she wonders whether this thing can all really fit into her.

I give her thigh a reassuring squeeze before I enter her.

"Aaahhhhh!" she cries out, clenching her eyes and grabbing a fistfull of sheets below her. She's tight around my cock. There's no way she's ever had something inside her as big as me. But at the same time, she's wetter than anyone I've ever been with, and she's so hot and slick that she can't be far from releasing already.

I lean forward so that her legs are back, far back, and I watch her chest rising and falling with each breath before I move my hands to her hips, and I start rocking back and forth.

When I entered her, I only thrust up halfway. The rest, I have to ease in, rocking it in inch by inch until I can feel my crown grinding against her vaignal walls.

In my first broad stroke of her insides, her eyes open wide with a gasp, and I know I've already found her g-spot. I'm past the point of being able to wait.

My hips start bucking into her, hard and fast. We've totally given into the lust of each other's bodies, and our tense, sensual exploring has become nothing but lustful rutting. My hips pound into her, and each thrust lets my cock roll up and down her pussy, which is wetting my cock to make it glide inside it like the two organs were made for each other.

Each pound earns me a whimpering breath from her. Her face is red, mouth open, and her hair is spread out to her side like a dark river.

My mind flits back to the sight of her fighting alongside me, handling herself like she would do well in *my* line of work. The sight of her ass as we moved through the hotel room together. Hell, the very sight of her when I first saw her in the doorway, hitting me like a freight train.

My cock stiffens harder than ever, and she cries out as I feel her orgasm tightening up in her before releasing, her cry of pleasure resonating throughout the soundproof room as I feel the slick wetness of her pussy get wetter around my cock. Her honey is all over my groin, her thighs, my ass, and the sheets as she comes, but I don't hold back or relent for a second.

I keep going.

I'm like a machine inside her, pounding with precise regularity, my heavy balls getting tight and needy with each thrust. I have control over myself so that I can make her lose all control.

"Oh god, Wes," she moans under me as I feel her legs on my torso, the warmth of her body on mine making us both glisten in the pale light of the safe room, our little hole in the world where nothing can intrude on us. "How...how are you...ohhhh!"

I can almost see her tightening and relaxing, the tension moving up her like a tide and leaving behind sweet bliss in every muscle, every inch of her body. Her orgasms leave her glowing more warmly than the cameras ever could.

Finally, when I've had my fun ruthlessly driving

her over the edge of orgasm, I slowly bring my bucking to a halt and slide my cock out of her.

She gives a whimper of protest, suddenly looking down at me with that pouting lip out. I let her legs fall to the mattress, and she finally winces from the effort of keeping her body so twisted around for so long.

"Not feeling tired already, are you?" I tease.

"Don't give yourself too much credit," she breathes, winking up at me.

"Careful, Miss Parker," my voice rumbles as I lower myself down to her wet lips, the heady smell of her passion in the air, "or you'll take on more than you can handle."

Before she can reply, I open my mouth and kiss her pussy, my tongue diving into her and tasting her sweet honey in a long, wet stroke.

Her whole body shivers in delight as she lets herself sprawl out and revel in the feeling of my tongue on her pussy. I stroke again and again, and the feeling of her inner thighs pressing against the sides of my head make my whole world a swirl of heat, lust, and sweet wetness.

I crave more of her. I grip her ass and bring her closer to me, holding her up against my face as she tosses her head back and lets her breaths come loud and freely as I feel her tension welling up again, her thighs getting tighter around me, and finally, I feel her release again, each of her orgasms coming more naturally than the last.

She twists her body and writhes to get away from me, breathing heavily as I raise my head and smile at her with a glistening mouth. My own chest rises and falls with slow, steady breaths. I'm in control, from start to finish.

And I'm not finished with her yet.

But I'm not cruel. I let her crawl back before I move forward onto her, sliding a hand under her neck and looming over her while my cock rests on top of her pussy. She shivers, a thrill running up her whole body from that sweet center, and her eyes open to look up at me.

There's wonder in her eyes. Maybe she can't believe she's really letting herself get fucked senseless by a guy she met less than a day ago. Maybe she's never had anyone make her feel this way. Maybe there's more in that gaze. It doesn't matter.

I gently rock my cock back and forth on her, making her slowly close her eyes again and lean her head back, moaning softly in the gentle motion.

After that, everything just becomes a dizzy haze of lust, like those moments early in the morning when you're in that strange world between dreaming and being awake. My cock is still stiff and hard, needy, my balls almost sore with need for Molly.

As for her, she never seems to stop moving. I

would have thought her to be totally worn out by now, but within a few minutes, her hips are starting to thrust up into me softly, quietly asking me for more. Her lips caress my shaft, reminding me of how good they feel, how tight she is around me.

When she starts running her fingers through my hair and looking up into my eyes, I smile down at her and kiss those lips that I've abused so terribly tonight.

"Ready for more?" I ask, my voice gravelly.

"I want to ride you," she pleads.

"You're brave."

"Tell me something I don't know."

My smile grows into a grin. I turn over onto my back--it's an awkward move, since this bed is so small compared to what she must be used to, but she manages to stay on top of me. Once I'm on my back, she turns her back to me and kneels down.

My cock is straight upright, and even though she isn't letting herself sit on me, it's already touching her sensitive lips, and I see her quiver.

She turns her head and looks down at me with lidded eyes, her hair half-covering the mischievous smile on her face.

"Don't get into something you can't handle," I warn her, raising an eyebrow at her boldness, considering how tight she was and how much of her I took up while on top of her.

"Worried?" she asks, a challenging edge to her voice.

"For you? Yeah," I growl, and the next moment, I put my hands around her hips and lower her onto me like a sheath around a sword.

Immediately, I feel her shudder around me in utmost pleasure, just as hot and wet as she was when we first started. She lowers her head, hair falling over her like a veil, but she tosses it back the next moment. The sight I get is that of her hair falling over her shoulders like a waterfall, ending in her round, firm ass that covers my cock.

Her ass is incredible. I'd take it as payment any day. The feel of it pressing against me as I lower her down to the hilt is worth a million words. And right now, it's all mine.

She starts trying to rock up and down, back and forth on my cock, but even with her on top of me, she finds that I'm in complete control. I hold her hips like reins, and I twist her any way I want her as I thrust my hips up into her. Each thrust leaves her almost helpless, and she looks like she's riding a mechanical bull as she tries to keep herself upright.

Her long legs are folded at my sides, trembling with the effort of everything she's done today. I thought the fight would wear her out, but we're getting more of a workout fucking each other into the night.

The tip of my cock grinds deeply against the

opposite side of her pussy this time, but each new part of her I feel gives me so much pleasure that I could burst at any second.

I could carry her all night like this, and I'm half-tempted to do just that. But this poor girl can't hold out much longer. The way things are going, I wouldn't be surprised if she wears me out at the same time.

I start thrusting upward harder, keeping a stronger grip on her hips and the soft skin around her waist. The actress's figure is so much more *real* than I was expecting, so human, so wonderful in every way.

And now, she's mine.

Before long, I'm pounding up into her savagely, less precisely than before, letting my momentum run totally wild. All poor Molly can do while I fuck her is use her hands to keep herself upright while I have my way with her, and I see her lips opening as she nears the edge of oragsm.

"Come in me, Wes!" she gasps suddenly, "fuck, I've- I've got to feel you in me!"

Irresponsible. Bad idea. Mistake. And sweet, messy release.

Thoughts race through my head like a storm, and it all comes crashing back to reality that this is an impulsive, spur-of-the-moment thing we're both doing, throwing caution to the wind...

...and it's that thought that makes my balls clench

up and my cock stiffen, poised, ready to release in just a few precious moments.

Those split-seconds between the point of no return and the big release have always been meaningful to me. It's as if a thousand thoughts fly through me all at once, so intensely, so sweetly.

This time, it's just the thought of Molly and that ass of hers that explodes a thousand times stronger in my head before a shot of white-hot seed erupts into her.

With the first shot, I realize that her whole body is shuddering around me, a full-body orgasm wracking her system. From the soft underside of my cock to the bulging tip and my whole pelvis, my my entire body feels the same intensity of the orgasm while shot after shot of my pearly fluid enters her, going deep into her body, warming her and mixing with her honey.

It's sloppy, exhausting, and completely blissful. The relief of my balls has never felt more fulfilling, more rewarding than when spilling into Molly Parker.

That's a thought I didn't think I'd be having by the end of today.

I reach up and take hold of her hair while more thrusts explode into her. I have so much seed that even she seems surprised by how long it takes for me to completely empty myself into her, to spend every last drop of myself in the sweetest pussy I've ever known.

Finally, when I've taken her completely, I let out a deep breath and release her hair, then her hips, and my arms fall to my side while my chest starts rising and falling in ragged, satisfied breaths.

I don't know how long we just stay there, my cock still hard inside her, my whole body relieved, hers a melting pile of gorgeous limbs and long hair stuck on top of me, both of us breathing heavily.

The room is thick with heat and sex.

What the hell did we just do?

Finally, I slide my hands to her hips, and she takes the cue to help get her off my cock, slowly, a sweet whimper of sensitivity coming from her lips as she gets off and falls next to me on the bed.

We stay there next to each other for a few moments before I look over at her, not knowing what to expect to see on her face.

I'm relieved to see the same uncertainty written all over the gaze she's giving me.

"Did we just do that?" she whispers, her voice ragged.

"We did, sweetheart," I say with my own boyish smile. "How do you feel about it?"

"I...I don't know," she says, sincere confusion in her quiet voice, "just that that's the best I've ever felt in as long as I can remember."

"Yeah," I say in agreement, and I see her cheeks blush at the thought that I feel the same way.

Jesus, how do we go from knowing exactly how to do everything with each other to not knowing where the hell to start with each other?

"Here," I say, rolling out of bed and walking to fetch a few cloths stored in the small room. I wet them in the warm water of the sink and take them to Molly and start to help clean her up, getting the sweat and traces of our lovemaking off her.

She doesn't resist when I run the warm towels over her body, nor when I get some fresh ones and dry her off. She just looks up at me with those huge eyes.

Finally, when she's dry and I start to wad the towels up, she stops me with a small hand on my wrist, and I look down at her. Her pleading eyes tell me everything, and I bend over to meet her in a soft kiss that makes my cock start to stiffen again.

Just what is she getting at?

When the kiss breaks, I smile down at her. "Careful, you won't get any sleep tonight acting like that."

That brings a smile to her dreamy face, and she looks down to the bed as if she forgot it was there. "Oh- oh right, I guess that's a thing we should do tonight, huh?"

"That's a thing *you* should do tonight," I say, starting to pull my clothes back on. "I'm your bodyguard, sweetheart. No letting my guard down for a little shuteye when you've got armed men looking for you, not even in the safe room. I'll keep an eye on things. You get some rest and..." *And think about whatever it was we just had together,* I think. "...well, get some rest," my gruff voice grunts.

She bobs her head absently, picking up her underwear a moment before giving up and tossing it aside, pulling the sheets over her.

I find a place to sit down and get comfortable with, but I feel myself being watched. I look over and see those amber eyes gazing at me, her face half-covered by the blankets.

I hold back a laugh. Her billboard was always staring down at me, and here she is again. I like it this way much better.

"Are you sure you can't sleep?" she says softly.

"Don't sweat it, Miss Parker," I say in a low, husky tone. "You've been through a lot tonight." I check the time on the wall, and I add, "By the way, merry Christmas."

I can make out a smile under the hair and blankets, and she murmurs "Merry Christmas" back to me.

Before long, I watch the blankets start rising and falling in a steady rhythm as she drifts into sleep.

Staying awake won't be a problem for me. I'm used to keeping watch late at night. Just not over such a stunningly beautiful prize like Molly.

I give my head a shake. What kind of thoughts

are those? She's a spoiled Hollywood starlet, a client, no more.

But I can't shake the nagging voice at the back of my head.

I'm starting to like this starlet.

I wake up to the sensation of someone gently stroking the hair back from my forehead and temples. I open my eyes slowly, feeling very heavy and exhausted. Like it's the morning after a particularly vigorous work out. As I blink, the room comes spinning into focus. That blank ceiling with the circular light. Gray walls. And it all comes rushing back to me.

Eddie. The hotel. The mercenaries. The roof. The safe room.

Wes.

Us. *Together.*

I sit up straight on the twin bed, eyes wide. Wes looks down at me, his arms folded over his chest. "Merry Christmas," he says flatly.

I groan, rubbing my hand over my face. "Yeah. You, too."

"How'd you sleep?" he asks, his voice a little softer now. Kinder.

I yawn and stretch, feeling the ache in my back. This mattress isn't exactly what I'm used to sleeping on. I shrug. "Okay, I guess. How about you?"

He walks away into the en suite bathroom. "I didn't."

"Didn't what?" I ask, swinging my legs over the side of the bed.

"Sleep. I'm your bodyguard, remember? We may be in a safe room but it's still in my job description to stay vigilant and watch out for you," he says.

"Oh," I murmur, feeling guilty and uneasy. There's something off in the air this morning. Something wrong. Like I've done something to tip the scales and now the whole world is just slightly off-balance.

Well, I think to myself, *you did fuck your bodyguard last night.*

Yeah. There's that.

"So what's the plan today?" I ask, getting up and walking over to lean against the wall next to the bathroom door, which is slightly ajar. I can hear Wes washing his hands, splashing water on his face. Probably trying to wake himself up and stay alert. I feel awful that he didn't get to sleep last night. It doesn't seem fair. If I had known he was going to stay up all night to keep watch, I would have at least offered to take the watch in shifts rather than just conking out for the night.

Wes comes out of the bathroom, drying his face with a towel. He's standing so close to me. Only a couple feet away. And already I can feel that electricity crackling between us like a downed telephone pole. I step aside instinctively, trying to reduce that burning tension.

"We can't stay here. I have a feeling your guy isn't just going to call off his goon squad because we're locked up here in this little hole in the ground. Hotel security has undoubtedly dealt with our two friends tied up on the roof by now. I wonder if they got to see Santa Claus last night from their vantage point," he says, smiling wryly. I can't help but smile, too. He's such a sardonic asshole, but god, he's gorgeous.

"Do you think he'll have someone waiting for us when we come out, though?" I ask nervously. He walks over and at first I think he's going to hug me, but instead he just pats my shoulder. Like he's my father or my soccer coach or something.

"You know Eddie Arnold better than I do," he says.

"Not as well as I thought I did," I answer somberly.

Wes reaches out and gently takes my chin in his hand, tilting my face up. He stares into my eyes, searching them. "I'm serious. Think about it. I know it's not what you want to think about right now, but if you have any insight into what that bastard might try next, you have to let me know. Okay?"

I nod, laying my hand on his and moving it to my lips, kissing it softly. He takes his hand back and turns away, walking over to the door. And just like that, the moment evaporates. Back to business, and I feel like an idiot. What the hell am I thinking, getting all sentimental and intimate with the guy hired to protect me? He's not here out of some emotional obligation. He's here because it's his damn job.

Normally, I am the epitome of professionalism. I've shared on-screen kisses with multiple costars, posed nearly nude with other models, and yet I have never felt even remotely tempted to pursue a romantic or sexual relationship with any of them. And I'm talking devilishly attractive, perfectly-in shape, wealthy actors and swimsuit models. Guys most women would die to meet. But something about Wes just... grabs me.

Yeah, and you need to get over it, I scold myself. This is not the time, nor the place, for me to get all soft and mushy about some random guy who's only here for a paycheck.

"Where are we going from here?" I ask, following Wes to the door.

He thinks it over for a minute, scratching at his beard. "I assume anywhere you normally frequent is going to already be on his watch list. If he's as organized and determined as he seems to be, there's a good chance he's thought ahead. He'll have your usual haunts completely staked out just in case you show up. Where do you normally hang out?" he asks me.

I can't help but snort at this question. He raises an eyebrow.

"What's so funny?" he says.

I shake my head. "I don't really do a lot of 'hanging out.' I'm a workaholic. If I'm not at the gym or on location filming, prepping for table reads, having business meetings-- then I'm either at the gym, the boxing studio, the self-defense classes, or at home," I explain.

"Okay. Well, that's already more locations than I go to in a regular week," Wes says. "Which will work in our favor, actually. The more places he needs to stake out, the more split up his people will be. Which means there will be less of them at any given location."

"It's crazy. I never even considered that Eddie might have, you know, guys on his payroll just waiting around to be sicced on someone like me. He just seemed so normal. Friendly, even. I mean, he's always been a bit of a schmoozer, and he can talk anyone into anything. But this is just... so not what I expected from him. I've known him all my life, Wes," I tell him sadly. "He's been like an uncle to me, and it turns out I never knew who the hell he was all this time."

"People can surprise you," Wes replies. "That's one thing I try to keep in mind, especially with this job. You may think you know somebody, but you never know what they might be hiding. Nobody shows their true selves anymore. It's all tucked away behind layers and layers of bullshit."

"Kind of a cynical perspective on the world, don't you think?" I comment.

He shrugs and types a code into the door. It slides open and the two of us walk back out.

"Better a cynic than a sucker," he quips back.

I can't really disagree with him on that, especially considering how my life has changed recently. It kills me to think that my family has been duped by Eddie Arnold all these years, led to believe he's a nice guy with good intentions. Jolly Uncle Eddie, always coming around to the house with little gifts and jokes and cutesy nicknames. Molly Pocket. Molly Golightly. Molly Pop. Acting like a big cuddly teddy bear when he's really just a snake in the grass. That now-familiar shame comes flooding back to me. I should have known. I should have seen it coming. I should have been more careful, more suspicious of his reasons for wanting to take me on as a client. Nobody ever does anything for good reasons these days, it seems like. Everyone's angling for some dark purpose.

Wes and I get in the special safe room-access elevator and take it to the lobby, where we quietly check out of the hotel and head outside into the brisk Christmas morning. We walk to the back parking lot and Wes brings me to his car, a black sedan with darkly-tinted windows, much like the car I arrived here in.

"Stand back for a few minutes. I need to check something," Wes commands, holding his arm out to stop me coming closer. I hang back, confused, as he performs a full check of the vehicle. He looks under the engine, at the undercarriage of the car, inside the driver's seat, behind the tires.

"What are you looking for?" I ask.

He stands up and brushes his hands off on his shirt. "Car bombs."

My heart skips a beat. "Oh."

"Looks clear. Let's get going," he says, climbing into the driver's seat.

I go around to the passenger seat and slide in. As we leave the parking lot, I turn to him and ask, "So, you never answered me. Where the hell are we going?"

"Somewhere you've never been before," he says.

"You could be more specific."

He smiles. "You ask way more questions than most of my clients."

"And you give worse explanations than most camera guys I've worked with," I shoot back, glaring sidelong at Wes. He glances over at me, a spark in his eyes.

"We're going to my place," he says simply.

"Are you sure? What if those guys are tracking me and your house gets compromised?"

He shrugs. "I'm not too attached to my apartment. It's nothing special. If I have to break a lease, I'll break a lease."

"How are you so calm about all this?" I ask.

"Well, apart from the fact that it's my job, I've seen much worse shit than this."

"Like what?" I press him. Wes sighs.

"Sorry. You have to get through about ten more layers of bullshit to get to that story," he says. "It's not a long drive, but if you're planning on firing questions at me the whole time, it'll feel a lot longer."

"Jeez. Sorry," I murmur. It's so weird. Last night, the two of us were on fire. So intimate. Entwined in each other's flames, desperate for touch, starving for closeness. And now, it's like we're back to how we were yesterday, snapping at each other like two kids scuffling on a playground at recess.

"God, I wish I could check in with Andie," I mutter aloud, leaning my head against the window. I need to know how Christmas is going. How well my parents took the lie Andie was supposed to feed them.

"Andie?"

"My little sister," I answer. "She's supposed to be covering for me at my family Christmas get-together. I'm worried about it." He nods.

"If you really need to, there are several burner phones in the dash compartment there," he instructs coolly. "That is, if you have her number memorized."

"I do," I say, quickly leaning forward and popping open the compartment. Indeed, there is a pile of simple, silver cell phones.

"Plug it in, charge it here," Wes says, gesturing to a long USB cord hanging out of the stereo console. I hastily attach one of the phones to the cord and turn it on. I wait impatiently for the load-up screen to pass, and then immediately fire off a text message to Andie. Her number is the only one I have memorized, purely because I use it so often.

"So… any particular reason you have a stash of burner phones hidden in your car?" I ask.

"Just because they're in a compartment doesn't make them *hidden*."

"Okay. Any reason why you have a stash of burner phones *not* hidden in your car?"

Wes laughs, a low, rough sound that sends a thrill through my body. Everything he does affects me. Every tiny movement. Every expression. Every word. I hate the hold he already has over me. We don't even know each other. Maybe this is just some bizarre offshoot of Stockholm Syndrome or something.

"My job requires a certain degree of secrecy, as you can probably imagine," he explains.

"Makes sense. I'll accept that answer," I tell him,

still staring down at the phone screen, desperately hoping for a reply from Andie.

"Good, because that's the only one you're getting," Wes comments.

We fall into silence, and I spend the rest of the drive alternating between staring out the window and staring down at the phone in my lap. By the time we cross town, sitting through about an hour of awful standstill Los Angeles traffic, and arrive at the apartment complex Wes calls home, I still haven't gotten a reply.

"We're here," he says, and we get out, walking up a couple flights of stairs to his apartment. Turning to me as he opens the front door, he adds, "Keep in mind, this is how the other half lives. My place makes that safe room look like Club Med."

"Oh, whatever. I'm not going to burst into flames just because you don't have valet service," I say, rolling my eyes as I walk past him into the apartment. When we get inside, I realize that he was definitely exaggerating. This place isn't anything special, nothing too showy or over the top, but it's certainly no hovel.

"I work a lot, so this place isn't exactly homey," Wes explains. "More of a crash pad."

"Still nicer than my studio apartment years ago," I tell him with a wink.

It's a small apartment with simple furnishings, unadorned white walls, smooth gray tile floors, and just enough furniture to make it comfortably livable. One bedroom, one small bathroom, a streamlined, simplistic kitchen. It suits Wes perfectly-- or at least, it suits whatever version of him I've seen so far.

"Well, make yourself comfortable. We've got nowhere to be and time to kill," he says, walking into the kitchen. "How do you like your coffee?"

"Black," I call after him.

"That's what I thought," he says in reply. I smile to myself and collapse on the sofa, still fiddling with the burner phone. The screen is blank. No answers yet. I try and urge myself to stay calm. There are a million reasons why Andie wouldn't answer quickly. She's at the Christmas celebration with my parents, and they, being the older generation, get a little grumpy when we get distracted by our cell phones during family time. She's probably only able to check her phone when she goes to the bathroom or something. And then there's the fact that she won't recognize the number I'm texting her from. Maybe she's just waiting to think it over and make sure it's really me messaging her. She's already doing me a huge favor by lying to our parents about where I am, so I shouldn't pester her too much.

Wes appears in the doorway holding a spatula. "So you like your coffee black, but how about your eggs?"

"Well, you seem to like guessing. So guess," I tell

him playfully. There I go again. Flirting with this guy who's just trying to do his job.

"Hmm. Over-medium with lots of black pepper?" he suggests.

"Wow. That's really specific--"

"Am I wrong?"

I laugh. "No. You're actually right."

He makes a fist pump and grins, looking like a handsome goofball. "Twice in a row!"

"Congratulations, you're officially psychic," I tell him, giggling.

"Bacon or sausage?" he asks.

"Surprise me," I answer.

"Adventurous," he remarks, disappearing into the kitchen again. A few minutes later I hear the clanging of pots and pans, the sizzle of breakfast in the skillet. I stretch out on the sofa, cradling the burner phone to my chest. Apparently, I'm comfortable enough to fall asleep, because I'm woken up some time later by the sound of a dish sliding onto the coffee table in front of me.

"I see how it is," Wes says, "You sleep all night and still catch a nap while I slave over a hot stove."

"I'm sorry," I say earnestly. "I have no idea why I fell asleep. I normally don't sleep at all during the day."

"It's a really comfortable couch," he says.

"You're a great cook. And a fantastic bodyguard. I mean, I never expected a meal out of the bargain," I comment, digging into breakfast. It occurs to me that neither of us have eaten in quite awhile, and my stomach growls plaintively. I check the time on the cell phone screen. It's already past noon.

"Don't get your hopes up. I'm pretty good at cooking breakfast, but lunch and dinner aren't as gourmet," Wes tells me. "I eat a lot of takeout."

"Maybe I'll cook dinner tonight," I mumble.

God, this is starting to feel like some bizarro domestic partnership.

"So how long are we hiding out here?" I ask, changing the subject.

"Until I hear from your lawyer that the coast is clear. Could take some time. I hope you didn't have any big work commitments planned out."

I sigh, poking the bacon around on my plate. "Doesn't matter. Eddie has all my offers on hold. I can't do anything until this whole thing is settled."

"Damn. He really fucked you over, didn't he?" Wes asks, his voice serious.

I nod slowly, feeling the anger rising up inside me. "Yeah. He really manipulated me. Played me like a fucking fiddle. I didn't see it coming, but I should have. I'm gullible. I'm an idiot. Is that what you want to hear?"

Wes sets down his fork and looks at me. Hard. For a second, I think he's going to be angry with me. Pick a fight. Tell me to shut up.

But instead, he just gets up and quietly walks

over to a record player in the corner of the living room, by the television. He takes an album out of the shelf nearby and places it under the needle. What the hell?

A moment later, the record crackles into a warm rendition of "Blue Christmas" by Elvis Presley. Wes disappears into the kitchen and then reemerges with a bottle of wine and two glasses. He pours a glass of red for each of us and then sits back down across from me at the coffee table. I give him a quizzical look.

"What's all that about?" I ask, confused.

He shrugs and takes a bite of his eggs and bacon, then a sip of wine. "It's Christmas."

Despite my sour mood, I burst out laughing. "It's not even one in the afternoon. Isn't that a little early for wine?"

"So, you're saying you *wouldn't* like a drink?" he asks, one eyebrow raised.

I hastily snatch up my glass of wine. "No. Not saying that at all."

"Look," he begins, "if we're going to get through this god-awful slumber party we've got ahead of us, we might as well try to make the best of it."

"And the Elvis?"

"Setting the mood."

I grin. "Just thinking about what you said earlier about how you can never really know anyone. You are full of surprises. I would never have pegged you for the kind of guy who would have an Elvis Christmas album in his collection."

He shrugs. "I'm from Vegas. Of course I've got Elvis."

As soon as the words leave his lips, his smile fades. Like he's instantly regretting having told me that little tidbit of information. I want so badly to pick at it, ask more questions, dig a little deeper. But I won't. It's not my place to push him.

So I change the subject. "This is so weird. You know, this is the first Christmas I have ever spent away from my family."

"How old are you?" he asks, a little snidely. He's still defensive.

"Ha-ha. I'm twenty-one. It's just that my family is really close. No matter where we all are during the rest of the year, no matter where work takes us and how busy we are, we always find a way to spend Christmas together. It's our tradition," I explain.

"That's sweet," he says.

"How about you?" I ask, and I can tell it's not a great question to ask him. There goes my plan of staying away from tricky topics. "Do you usually go home for Christmas?"

"No. I haven't been home in… a while. This is home now. Right here," he says brusquely. I nod and sip my wine, feeling guilty. I never thought I was an overly inquisitive person until I met Wes. But something about him just interests me. Makes me want to know more about him. Who he really is.

"I don't know if this year would have been much fun for me at the Christmas get-together anyway," I go on. "Not with what's going on."

"Really? It seems like you would want to be with your family right now. Have your support system readily available."

I nod, smiling sadly. "Yeah. Normally, I would. But things are... awkward with my parents at the moment. You see, Eddie is their oldest and best friend. He's been like a family member for all my life. We all trusted him. Completely. And when I told my parents what happened between us, well... they had a hard time visualizing the event."

Wes sets down his wine glass, frowning. "What does that mean?"

"Just that they, I don't know, couldn't quite believe what I told them."

"You mean, they sided with him?"

I shrug. "Not exactly. More like they were just confused, I guess. And I was already so upset that when they didn't immediately listen to me, I just kind of stormed out. I was so hurt. And angry. And now they probably think I'm skipping the Christmas party just because I'm mad at them or something."

"You have every right to be mad at them," Wes says forcefully. "They're your parents. They're supposed to have your back. Under any circumstances. Family is… everything."

I'm a little surprised at the vitriol in Wes's tone. He seems genuinely worked up about this whole thing. In a way, it's validating. "Yeah. You're right."

"What did he do to you, anyway?" he pushes.

I idly swirl the contents of my wine glass around, trying to think of how to word it.

"Eddie?"

"Yeah, of course, Eddie. What happened?" Wes asks, leaning forward.

I can't meet his eyes somehow. "He just made a move on me. That's all. It's such a stupid thing. It happened so quickly. We were just having a normal business meeting, and then suddenly, his hand was on my thigh and he was trying to kiss my neck and… I just got up and ran out. I couldn't even process it at first. I kept thinking I imagined it. But I didn't. It was real. It happened. And it's all been downhill from there," I describe quietly.

"Jesus, Molly," Wes swears. "That's…" He trails off, just staring at me for a long moment. Then he picks up the bottle of wine and refills both our glasses. I give him a smile of gratitude.

"Thanks."

"You're one tough woman, you know that?" he says, shaking his head. I blush. "I'm serious. Most women would probably have just let him do what he pleased. Suffered in silence. It takes a lot of courage to stand up to a guy like Eddie Arnold. Especially with his relationship to your family."

"Well, thank you, I guess," I answer, smiling weakly. "I just wish this shit would all blow over so I could get back to work and think about something else for a change. It's killing me, just sitting around with a target on my back, just waiting to see what that bastard does next."

There's a long silence between us, the air trembling with the sweet sound of the vinyl album circling. Then, Wes speaks up. "You know. There are some things we could do to take your mind off of it. Just for a little while."

I look up at him. Those eyes, blazing brightly again.

Coaxing me. Promising me bliss. Ignorance. A welcome distraction.

I shouldn't. We shouldn't. But god… I want to.

There's hesitation in her eyes, and I'm ready to back off at a moment's notice. Maybe I've been misreading things between us, and what happened at the hotel was just what it was--a quick, impulsive thing done in the heat of the moment.

But then I see that hesitation give way to the dancing, curious fire behind her amber irises that hit me the first time I looked into them.

"What do you have in mind?" she asks, her voice smooth with feigned, inviting innocence. Her fingers stroke a lock of her hair, twisting one around her finger idly, and it hits me that she's nervous.

Molly Parker. Nervous.

She isn't even in mortal danger this time.

The thought brings an amused smile to my lips.

Without another word, I move forward and scoop her up into my arms. She yelps in surprise, but she puts her hands behind my neck to hold on as if she were expecting it the whole time.

She giggles as I bounce her lightly in my arms as I turn around, and while I start carrying her back to the bedroom, I kiss her on the neck, making her recoil and squirm in my arms while I squeeze her ass.

Music follows us back to the room, and I push the door open with my ass as I hear her shoes fall to the floor with a clatter.

"Here I thought actresses were supposed to be composed all the time," I tease her, whispering into her ear.

"Some of us like to live a little," she says.

Instead of tossing her down on the bed, this time I sit down with her, holding her in my arms, letting her curl into my lap and wiggle her ass into my legs, making me stiff in a matter of seconds. My cock remembers how her ass feels, even through jeans, and I'm hungry for more.

But this time is more measured, less impulsive. I'm going to take my time with her. Enjoy her body as much as she enjoys mine.

My rough hand moves up and down her back. I let my thumb feel her shoulderblades, run down the bones of her back, feeling her through her skirt. Her eyes are burning holes in me, and I'm lost in them.

The next moment, with incredible dexterity, she swings a leg up over me so that she straddles me, wrapping her legs around my waist and letting me hold her sides while she tosses her hair back.

"You're getting fond of that position," I point out.

"I'm a creature of habit sometimes," she says, a light blush coming to her cheeks. I reach up and run my hands through her hair and start playing with it, watching the dark locks run smoothly down my hands. She seems to like that, so I go further into her hair, my whole hand getting lost in her while she sighs contentedly, melting into me until her face rests against my shoulder.

When I feel like it's getting too sleepy for my liking, I lean in and kiss her neck again, my beard tickling her skin and making her wiggle again on me and playfully squirm back. I hold onto her tight to keep her from escaping, but when she takes her hands off my shoulders, I take the moment to lift her shirt up over her head and toss it aside, leaving her once more naked before me.

I cup one of her breasts in my hand, running my thumb over the soft, expensive fabric with a thoughtful smile. "How much did this thing cost?"

"They're expensive," she says with a roll of her eyes.

"I can't imagine how much they can get away with for a Hollywood wardrobe."

"They're unbelievable at a regular store," she says

pointedly. "The bra industry could fund a whole movie if it wanted to."

"Sounds like a conspiracy in the making," I say in a gruff, serious voice with a raised eyebrow, and she giggles. With a quick motion, I unhook the bra and toss it to the floor, leaving her whole torso exposed to me.

A satisfied rumble comes from my chest as I devour her with my eyes, running my hands up and down her back as she watches me take her in. There's a smug satisfaction on her face and in those lidded eyes.

"I'm starting to think you like getting felt up by a scruffy vagrant like me," I say, cocking my head to the side and narrowing my eyes.

"Only as much as you like getting your hands on a 'spoiled starlet'?" she quips with a wink that hits me through the heart, and I give a deep, rumbling chuckle before I lean her back in my arms and put my lips to her nipple.

She gives a faint gasp as I run my tongue around her areola and flick the tip of her nipple. I can feel her heartbeat under her skin as I toy with her, getting her stiffer, running my hands up and down her back. I dig my hands into her, nails scratching softly along that sensitive, pampered skin while I take her nipple between my teeth gently.

It's stiff by now, and I move to the other stiffening bud and play with it, Molly's quivering form helpless in my hands. I can't lie, the feeling of having her in my grasp like this is something I could get used to.

My teeth graze her carefully, perilously close to the most sensitive parts of her breasts. Her skin is smooth and softer than I could have possibly imagined before I felt them. I want to ravage her immediately, but instead, I think it better to ease into it this time.

"You've been through a lot," I whisper in a husky tone. "You need to unwind."

"Didn't know that was in a bodyguard's job description," she says as she runs her fingers through my hair, holding the back of my head while I devour her breasts.

"You're not the only one full of surprises," I growl back at her. At that, she looks up, a faint smile on her face. I feel her pause, and I look up, arching an eyebrow.

"What?"

"Nothing," she says, going a little red in the cheeks. I grin, then lean forward and press a kiss into her lips. The kiss turns fierce, her hands going to my strong jaw and pulling her forward, pressing her breasts to my chest before they go down to the hem of my shirt, tugging at it.

I oblige, pulling the shirt off and leaving myself exposed before her.

She runs her hands over my broad chest, those

kissable lips curling up into a smile with a satisfied murmur while I feel her soft palms touching me, appreciating my hardened, chiseled form.

"This is my favorite surprise, I think," she muses, feeling my chest hair and squeezing my shoulders, and I feel quiet pride swelling up inside me. "Maybe I should use bodyguards more often."

"Oh?" I say, a challenged look on my face. "I think you'll find my rates very competitive."

She giggles and leans in to kiss me, and I run my hand possessively down her back. "I've got another surprise you might enjoy though," I say, a thought coming to me, and she tilts her head curiously.

Suddenly, I stand up, carrying her with her legs around my waist, and she holds onto my neck while I carry her into the bathroom.

Inside, I have the one feature of the house that I'm a little bit ashamed to admit to having. Molly's eyebrows go up at the sight of a very large garden tub in the corner of the bathroom, pristine and unused.

"You've got to be kidding me," Molly says, biting her lip to hold back a smile. "I had you pegged for a standing-shower kinda guy with a tumbleweed instead of a sponge.

"This came with the apartment," I say. "Too expensive to get rid of, so I just leave it the way it is. Haven't used it a single time.

"Then why's there a travel bottle of bath oil on the edge of it?" she asks, fast as lightning, and I feel my back stiffen. She grins triumphantly at me while my face goes a little red.

"...okay, that was a lie. That came with a congratulations-on-your-first-job package my friend Cody sent me. I used it once with a cold beer to celebrate on my own."

"Awww," she gushes, leaning her head into me, and I roll my eyes. "You know I'm literally never letting you live that down, right?"

"Uh-huh," I grunt.

I set her down long enough to start the water running, and while she strips her clothes off, I pour the rest of the little bottle in with the hot water and dispose of the evidence.

And I have to admit, the oils make the room smell pretty nice.

Once there's enough water in the tub, I strip my own clothes off and turn to see Molly leaning against the bathroom sink, utterly naked.

My heart rate picks up, and she smiles at the effect the very sight of her has on me. Her nipples are still stiff from my toying with them, and I notice her eyes are looking at my half-erect cock between my legs, hanging brashly and only getting stiffer at the sight of her.

She approaches me, and I take her into my arms,

her naked flesh electrifying my touch. She's warm and soft as I am hard, and it's so natural when I scoop her up and lower her into the bath that I'd think I'd been doing it for years, if I didn't know better.

It's almost surprising how natural, how *right* it feels.

I climb into the tub with her, and my bulk takes up a huge amount of space. It almost feels small once I get in, and Molly giggles at how much the water rises as I settle down into it.

"Are you sure this thing came with the apartment? Looks like it's a perfect fit for you."

"Shut up," I say with a grin as I get comfortable, and I use my legs to push her around the edge of the tub to slide her into me, and I wrap my arm around her.

She sighs contentedly once the water rises over her chest and up to my midriff, and she nestles into my side, leaning her head against my shoulder with her hair draped over the edge of the tub so it doesn't get wet.

"So, it may not be the luxury you're used to," I say, "but it's cozy, yeah?"

"It's new, believe it or not, and it's exactly what I need," she says, reaching up and putting a hand on my chest, feeling my slow, steady heartbeat.

We relax for a few moments, letting our thoughts drift to nowhere before I break the silence. "So wait, what do you mean, 'new'? I thought starlets like you did this kind of thing constantly."

"Have a legitimately private moment all to yourself and someone you like to just unwind with no pretenses for as long as you like?" she asks, raising an eyebrow at me. "You're kidding, right?"

I give her a look that definitely does not suggest kidding.

She shakes her head. "Everything's either too busy or too scripted for me. Always has been for my family. This one time, we went on a little vacation to Maui at this big 'private' resort, and even then, there were photo ops all the time. I was just trying to hang out with my sister or my parents, and we were either getting pulled off to pose or having to move to avoid the paparazzi that weren't supposed to be there."

I raise my eyebrows, genuinely surprised. "Wow."

"Yeah," she muses, looking a little sad. "Wow."

I squeeze her side and look down at her with a smile. "Well, you're incognito for a little longer, at least. Might as well enjoy it while we have the chance."

She smiles up to me, a sunny smile that makes me feel my cock start to harden under the sweet-smelling waters, and it isn't long before I have to bend down and kiss her. Our naked bodies pressed together, we can't keep our hands off each other for much longer.

The next second, my hands are on her hips and

hers are on my shoulders. Our lips are pressed against anywhere they can find, tongues dancing together, legs intertwining. I don't know how long we're in that bath tub, but it feels like hours, even though it was probably only twenty minutes at most. My hands grope her ass, her breasts, feel her chin, any part of her I can find. Every inch of her is like touching heaven.

She takes her time with my body, too, counting my abs, running her hand along my cock from base to tip and making it stiffen as much as she likes, holding my balls in her hands and whispering things into my ear that get my blood stirring.

No wonder I eventually have enough of it all, and I stand up, holding her in my arms as I carefully step out onto the tile and towel us off briefly before rushing us out the door.

I feel like we're teenagers sneaking around, and my heart is pounding as I chase her into the bedroom, her bubbly laughter making my heart skip. She leaps onto the bed, and I'm right after her, putting a knee on the bed and pinning her down with my arms, our faces just a few inches apart as she beams up at me, hips squirming, and I realize that this is the real Molly Parker--the human, not the actress. Her guard is down, and she's in front of me with intentions as naked as her body.

As I lean forward, I feel the tip of my erect cock

touch her lips, and I feel that she's as wet as the first time we fucked each other in the safe room.

An unspoken question hangs in the air between us, our faces so, so close.

Are we doing this again, with clear heads and unfettered lust?

Blue. The deepest ocean blue I've ever seen outside of the beach. It's such a magical, almost unnatural color that it's hard to believe it's real. I feel like if I could just let go of this world, with all its pain and stress and fear, I could give in, just fall forever into that lovely blue until nothing matters anymore. Until everything is gone, melted away. No work. No struggle to stay relevant. No picking apart my appearance in the mirror, high-lighting the flaws a casting director might hone in on and mark me as unusable, un-castable. No Eddie, pulling the strings and turning me into a terrified, trapped marionette doll at his mercy. I wish I could just float away from all of that. Wes is gazing at me with those luminous eyes, asking so many questions without breathing a word. Offering me a chance, a life preserver drifting in the open sea.

Take me. Set me adrift. Let me float away with you, far from all this mess.

I open my lips, just barely. A plea catches itself in my mouth, hanging there, afraid to stumble out and ruin everything with a few words. Words are so limited. Even when you think so hard about what to say and how to say it, when you dig through a thesaurus and a dictionary and wrack your brain for the best sequence of syllables to make yourself understood-- words fall short. No matter what you say, the meaning gets stuck in traffic.

I don't want him to ask me if it's okay. I want him to just *know*. I see that recognition in his stare. He does know. He understands. It's clear, this magnetism between us. The electricity is so powerful that I'm surprised we haven't short-circuited every appliance in the apartment. He has to know that I already belong to him, that he could bend me and break me into pieces if he wanted to and I would let him. Maybe it's just that I'm vulner-able right now, with my whole career and maybe even my life itself dangling by a thread. Maybe it's just because it's been so, so long since someone touched me with an ounce of the kind of passion and intensity that Wes does. Maybe it's just because there's nothing else I can think of to do right now besides this.

Or maybe it's because there is something greater

than just sexual energy between us, and we're both terrified and exhilarated at the mere thought of it.

The reason doesn't matter. I'm his for the taking, and I know he knows it.

So why is he hesitating?

"Molly," he breathes. His voice is a low growl, like gravel in his throat. Like he's struggling to hold himself together as he hovers over me, those blue eyes piercing me straight through to the sheets. The sound of my name on his lips makes me shiver. Tiny goosebumps spread along my bare skin. His eyes flit over my arms and chest, taking in the sight, watching what his voice alone can accomplish. Marveling in the effect he has on me.

I give him a soft smile, swallowing hard in anticipation of what might happen next.

He bends slowly to kiss me, his teeth barely grazing my bottom lip. I can tell he's calling upon every last shred of self-control to restrain himself. To take it slow. But he doesn't have to. He doesn't need to treat me like a delicate piece of china. I'm durable. Strong. And even if he does break me, I'm ready for it. I'm desperate for it.

I moan into his mouth, rolling my hips upward against him. Every muscle in his body is tightening up, tensing to stay in control. It's all he can do to keep from grabbing me and ravishing my body, using me. How can I tell him to go ahead? That there are things I am so afraid of in this world, but he is not one of them? There might have been a time when I would shy away from this. Recoil and withdraw, run away back to my lonely condo and lick my wounds in private. Tell myself in the mirror that I don't want it. I don't need it.

Tell myself I can do without love. Without passion. After all, it's just another pretty distraction from work, isn't it? Just another weight to slow me down.

But even if it may be true, it doesn't matter to me now. My career is being held captive in Eddie Arnold's greasy hands. I can't work. I can't plow away into the future. I can't put on those blinders that keep me moving forward without ever glancing back or taking time to watch the world slide by around me.

All I have, all I want right now is here. In this room. Underneath the watchful gaze of the bluest eyes I've ever seen. Wes pulls back and sweeps the hair back out of my face, looking at me like he's seeing me for the very first time. And it's that expression on his face that finally gives me the courage to say the words I've been holding onto.

"Don't make me wait anymore," I whisper. "I know what I want."

Wes kisses me again, fiercely, his tongue probing into my mouth while his hands rove down my face. Down my neck, my arms, and back up to my breasts. He cups them in his hands, the calloused skin rough and ticklish on my sensitive flesh. He bites my lip, not deep enough to draw blood, but deep enough to hurt. I can feel that warmth between my legs getting hotter, tingles rolling from my head to my toes. He unfolds me like a flower, blooming under sunny blue skies. I spread my legs for him, arching my back to press my breasts into the cups of his hands. He massages them, squeezing gently, then rolling his thumbs and forefingers over my nipples until they stiffen into peaks. I groan, tossing my head back as he bends to tug a nipple between his teeth. He flicks his tongue over it, sucking and squeezing until I'm panting with need. Tendrils of sharp pleasure reverberate through me, making my clit ache. I need him to touch me there. I need his hand or his mouth or his cock. Badly.

Almost as though he can read my mind, he slides a hand down along my stomach, over my pelvis, to cup my mound, using his middle finger to stroke my slick sex. I thrust into his hand involuntarily, instinctively pushing toward that glorious touch. His fingertip brushes over my clit and I cry out, trembling. I reach my arms out and grab hold of the sheets, steadying myself. He lifts his fingers to his lips and sucks my sweet juices from them, his eyes closing tight in pure enjoyment. He leans back down, kissing his way up between my breasts, along my collarbone, to that ticklish spot on the side of my neck. I shiver, torn between wanting to pull away and wanting to stay in this position forever. He kisses lightly at first, just letting his teeth brush over the skin, and then he sucks harder. One hand cups my left breast, stroking my nipple and squeezing the taut, smooth flesh, and his other hand slips down between my thighs. He circles my clit with two fingers, making me burn and shake.

"Oh god, oh god," I murmur breathlessly, my eyes rolling back in my head.

Wes sucks a deep, bruising kiss into my neck, making a mark on me to brand me as his own. I almost can't wait to look in the mirror later and see what it looks like. See the purple proof that Wes fucked me, took control of me, marked me for however long the bruise lasts. I wish I could keep it forever, remind myself every time I pass a reflection that I was his. That I will probably always be his. Because right now, in this overwhelming, pulsing tidal wave of emotion and passion, I know. I know I'm his.

Wes knows it, too. I can tell by the way he plays me like a beloved guitar, his fingers slipping over my skin like he knows me by heart. He finds those sensitive, hidden places so easily, by instinct, reading me from memory or by some crazy psychic connection. Whatever it is, I never, ever want him to stop.

He slips a finger inside me, hooking it to stroke expertly at that most hidden of gems deep within. His lips rove down to suck my breasts again, licking and biting gently at my nipples. I rock my hips and moan, unable to even think of a coherent sentence, much less say one. My pleasure is mounting, circling around that little knot of bliss he's building inside me, making it almost hurt, it's so fucking good. I whimper, gripping the sheets tightly.

"Yes, baby," he growls, looking up at me. "Come for me. I want to feel your sweetness all over my hand. Give it to me, sweetheart. I know you need this."

I rock against his hand a few more times and then I come with a shattering scream, collapsing like a ragdoll as my pussy clenches and twitches around his fingers. Wes bends to kiss me, biting and sucking as he positions the head of his thick cock at my pulsing hole. I wrap my legs around his waist, pulling him closer, begging him to fuck me.

"Tell me how you want it," Wes commands, those blue eyes flashing with danger.

"Hard. Please, Wes. Fuck me hard. I want it… I want it to hurt," I beg him. "Fill me up."

He teases me for a moment, rubbing the head of his shaft in a tight circle around my pussy, tantalizing me, making me desperate. I thrust up toward him and he smirks. There's no question who is in control, and it sure as hell isn't me. Normally, that might scare me. I like to be in control. I'm always taking charge. But not now. Not with Wes. I don't have to. He knows just what I need and how to give it to me. It's liberating. Freeing.

And it's fucking hot as hell.

"I'm gonna fuck you until you're screaming, but don't you dare come until I tell you to," Wes orders. "Got it?"

I nod. "Yes. Yes," I manage to whisper.

"Good girl," he hisses through gritted teeth. And then he pushes the full, enormous length of his cock inside me, sliding in to the hilt. I whimper and clench around him, my pussy convulsing instantly at the overwhelming pleasure. He's so fucking big. I can feel myself stretching to accommodate him. It hurts, in the best way possible.

"Fuck me, Wes. God, I need you to fuck me," I plead. He wraps his arms around my thighs and moves backward, yanking me to the edge of the bed as he stands up, his shaft still feeling sheathed inside me. He hooks my legs over his shoulders, slides a pillow under my ass, and with his hands gripping the soft flesh of my thighs, he starts to thrust. At this angle, I can feel everything-- every last glorious inch of his massive cock slamming into me, striking my g-spot over and over again.

"Oh, fuck," he groans. "Such a tight little pussy."

He fucks me so hard I can feel my body sliding up on the bed, but he pulls me back, snapping his hips to shove his cock in and out faster and faster.

"Touch yourself. Play with your clit, sweetheart. I want to see you writhe."

Obediently, I reach down and start to massage my clit, moaning at the near-incomprehensible bliss of stimulating my clit and my g-spot at the exact same time. Wes smirks devilishly, licking his lips at the sight of me, like I'm the most delicious thing he's ever seen in his life. He fucks me deeply, grabbing hold of my hips and lifting me up to slam into me harder while I tremble and whimper. I can feel my orgasm coming closer, my pussy tightening up as Wes pounds into me.

"You want to come, don't you, baby?" he growls.

I nod. "Yes. Oh, fuck. Please. I need to come," I breathe.

"Not yet. I'm not finished with you yet," he promises darkly.

He reaches down and scoops me up. I put my arms around his neck as he holds me up, his strong arms bouncing me up and down on his cock, spearing me so deeply it almost feels like he might break me in half. Face to face now, he kisses me, swallowing back every single one of my moans. My climax is getting closer and closer now, stimulating further by that deep ache.

"You ready, sweetheart?" Wes whispers in my ear, sending shivers down my spine.

"I'm ready. Please," I gasp.

"Come for me, baby. Come all over my cock," he

demands. He fucks me faster, holding me up and bouncing me on his shaft harder.

And just like that, I'm screaming, going limp as I gush all over him, making us slippery as he lowers me back onto the bed. He stands up and snaps his fingers. "Turn around. Get on your hands and knees like you did in that air vent. Show me that beautiful ass," he commands.

Still pulsing from the waves of orgasm, I do what he orders, bending over and looking back at him over my shoulder eagerly. At this point, he could tell me to do absolutely anything and I would do it in a heartbeat. As long as he keeps making me come, he can have anything in the world he wants. I have never felt like this before, and I don't want it to end.

Wes grabs me by the hips and shoves his cock back inside my trembling, slick pussy easily, starting out slow for a second before picking up the pace. He bounces my ass against him, his balls slapping against my clit as he buries his cock deep within me.

"Such a good girl, taking every fucking inch," he groans, fucking me so hard it brings tears to my eyes. "I think you deserve to come again, don't you?"

"*Fuck*-- oh god-- yes! Yes!" I exclaim as he pounds into me, stuffing me full of his shaft.

He reaches underneath me to stroke my clit, rubbing his fingers in tight circles around and around while his cock shoves into my g-spot, hit after hit. I can feel my body going all tingly and tense, building toward another orgasm. Wes slaps my ass, then squeezes it tightly with his free hand, using it to steady himself as he fucks me faster and faster. I can feel him starting to lose control, the rhythm getting more and more erratic. I clench my pussy around him, squeezing him tight and making him groan.

"Yes, Molly. Just like that, sweetheart. You want me to come inside you, don't you? Just stuff you with my come?" he rumbles, rolling my clit between his fingers until I'm seeing stars.

"Oh--oh, fuck-- yes. Yes! Wes, oh god!" I cry out.

"Yeah, baby. Tighten that little cunt for me," Wes groans.

"Feels-- so-- fucking-- good," I whine, falling forward and burying my face in the sheets while he pounds me so hard from behind, his hand gripping my ass, bruising me, marking me as his own just the way I like it…

"Molly!" he bellows, and he tightens up for a moment just before letting his thick seed pour deep inside my pussy. Scarcely a half-second later I'm wailing, pulsating around him and gushing sweet honey all over his cock as he fucks into me a few more times, milking every last drop of his come into me. Both exhausted, he pulls me up to kiss the back of my neck, wrap his arms around me, his hands squeezing my breasts as we cling together through the last dazzling waves of shared pleasure.

He releases me and slides out, climbing onto the bed beside me as we collapse against the pillows. Still shaking, I wriggle into his arms, resting my forehead against his powerful chest while his muscular arms slide around me, shielding me from the world. Here, in this moment, nothing can hurt me. No pain in this world can reach me. With Wes, I'm safe.

We stay this way for the rest of the night, curled up on the bed, soaking in the warmth of each other's presence. We don't need words. We don't need anything but this, just being together in the comfortable silence. I'm exhausted, and Wes hasn't slept in twenty-four hours. For a moment, he acts like he might get up, go post up and keep guard. But I pull him closer, unwilling to let him go for even a second. The moon casts glowing pillars of light through the windows while the city goes to sleep outside. Just before I drift off to sleep, I reach out and grab my burner phone. There's still no answer from my sister. I know I should be worried, but I'm so fucking tired, so comfortable here with Wes, ready to sleep.

But before I close my eyes, I send a quick SOS text message to Andie.

IN THE MORNING, I wake up still wrapped in Wes's arms, my whole body aching with the effort of last night's fuck. I roll over and kiss him gently on the nose and those bright blue eyes flutter open. He smiles, warming my heart.

I slowly sit up, stretch, and then instinctively check the burner phone. It dawns on me, the memory of sending that SOS message to Andie last night. I click the screen open, and my heart stops. There's still no answer. Andie has never ignored an SOS message. Ever. Something is horribly, horribly wrong.

"You need to stay calm right now," I say as I pull my jacket on.

Molly isn't on the same wavelength.

She's been pacing back and forth for the past five minutes, checking her phone repeatedly as if she's trying to make sure she hasn't just missed a message or is reading something wrong.

And in all honesty, I don't think her fears are unfounded.

"I can't," she snaps, brushing a lock of hair out of her face yet again. "I need to figure out what to do, I-I-I can't just sit around and do nothing, there's no way that Andie wouldn't be answering unless there was something seriously, seriously wrong!"

"I believe you," I say, nodding firmly and making eye contact with her. "But we can't do anything until we have a clear head and think things through step by step."

"We don't have time!" she nearly shouts, stopping at the kitchen counter and leaning back on it, consciously trying to keep herself from biting her nails. She wrings her hands instead. "But I'm on the run, I'm supposed to be staying under the radar, there are fucking *mercenaries* after me! That fucking bastard Eddie has to have something to do with this, he *has* to!"

"He could be trying to lure you out," I point out, crossing my arms. "He must know the two of you are close. If he wants to get to you or draw you out somehow, this is easily the best way to do it."

She nods in agreement, but the worry on her face only gets worse. "That doesn't help either of us though. Fucking...fuck!" she walks in a circle in the kitchen, putting her hands on her hair before forcing herself to take a breath. "That fucking bastard."

It's a dirty play--and it's one that I recognize. It's the kind of thing the mafia does all the time, and I've known people who have done similar things personally.

"So if I try to find her, I'm just putting myself out there for Eddie to find, but if I don't, Andie's in trouble, but even if Eddie isn't behind it, I'm supposed to be keeping a low profile and and and-"

"Molly!" I say, stepping forward and putting my hands on her shoulders gently, squeezing them and looking into her eyes. They're wild and panicked, so I keep a calm as face as I can. "You need to get a hold of yourself. Follow my breaths," I say, and together, we practice breathing--five seconds in, seven seconds out, several times, until Molly's hands have stopped shaking.

While we breathe, my mind races with possibilities. My instinct is just to keep her here and keep my client safe. That's the responsible, professional thing to do.

I've broken all kinds of professional boundaries in the past two days, though.

I know my feelings for Molly--whatever that means--are affecting my judgment, but that aside, I know there's a good chance her fears are very valid. And I know Molly enough by now to know that she won't stay put in peace. She's better than that.

"Alright," I say once I see the panic settle down in Molly's eyes. "My professional opinion is that we should work backward from what you know about Andie's whereabouts. It's the day after Christmas. Who would Andie have talked to recently?"

Molly gives a frustrated sigh and breaks away from me, pacing into the living room. "I have no idea. She has a huge network of people she could be in touch with, we both do. She's always out with someone."

That makes Molly pause, and I can see why. I step into the living room with her.

"Okay, so it would be unusual for her to be alone."

"...but if something happened to her and I don't know about it yet, then it was either someone close to her who did it," she winces at the thought, "or she was alone for some reason."

"Right," I say, nodding. "So, do either of those options ring a bell?"

"I...can't imagine," she says, shaking her head. "She should have been with my parents on Christmas Eve, but I don't know what her plans for the next day were. She can't have been with my parents, because they had plans on their own, and we aren't that close with the rest of the family. Most people don't work around Christmas, so that rules out most of the work contacts, unless there was something going on she wasn't telling me."

"Does she live alone?" I ask.

"No," she says. "She lives with a couple of other models--Stella and Taylor. They're about her age, but they don't do anything on screen, I don't think, they're full-time models."

"So not likely suspects," I say.

"God no," she says. "I'd try to get in touch with them, but they're definitely out of town for Christmas. I remember Andie saying something about the apartment being empty for a little bit and giving her some breathing space."

I nod. "So we don't have any leads and don't know who she might have talked to last."

"And it's the day after Christmas," she adds, slumping on my couch and burying her face in her hands, "so anyone who works in information is probably shut down still."

We're silent for a few moments before I bring up the elephant in the room that's only obvious to me. "Well, that leaves us with one obvious option."

She looks up, and I look down at her.

"But you're not gonna like it."

"IF SOMEONE FINDS out about this, I'll never live it down."

I smile. "Then we'll be careful."

We're driving up to the security guard box at the gate of the neighborhood where Andie and her roommates live.

We're on our way to break into her apartment.

Molly is wearing the closest thing to a disguise we could pull up on short notice. It's nothing more than a celebrity might usually wear around the Hollywood area, just...not exactly fitted. I put her in one of my jackets, hilariously oversized, and I put a pair of huge sunglasses on her.

She looks like she just got finished with one hell of a night.

"Don't think I don't see you trying not to laugh at me," she hisses as the security guy waves to us.

I just smile, saying nothing.

"Don't worry about this guy," she adds, nodding to the guard. "I have a feeling he's not involved in high intrigue."

"Can I help you two?" the man says as we stop at the gate, rolling down the window. He's a short man with a mustache, and I can hear a soap opera playing from a little TV in his box. I start to say something, but Molly leans over me and raises her sunglasses.

"Hey, Hal," she says with a wink. "Just dropping off a Christmas present a little late--don't tell on me, okay?"

"Well hey there Miss Parker!" he says with a broad smile. "Secret's safe with me. Merry late-Christmas."

He goes back into his box and opens the gate for us, and Molly gives him a wave as we go.

"Quick thinking," I remark as we pull through the rich neighborhood with beautifully maintained streets.

"There's a reason actresses made great spies in World War II, you know," she says. "Never underestimate someone who's been trained in improv."

"I'll try to remember that."

Molly points out the building where Andie and her roommates live, and I pull the car to a stop in what she tells me is her usual parking spot. There's nobody there. That makes Molly nervous, so I don't bring it up.

"I'm guessing you don't have a key?" I ask as we get out of the car.

"Never got one made," she says, her eyes widening. "Shit, you weren't relying on that, were you?"

I raise an eyebrow at her. "You don't think I would have asked by now?"

She flashes a smile at me. "I figured you'd be relying on me for everything by now."

I smirk back, shaking my head as I head toward the apartment. She follows after me, taking the glasses off and tucking them into the huge jacket. "Okay, but seriously, what *is* the plan?"

I don't answer. Instead, I just head straight for the hallway under the buildings, outside the apartment building, until I find a set of doors. "Utility room," I say simply.

"What about it?" she asks, following at my heels while I look around us before going to the door.

I take out a hairpin and start fiddling with the lock.

"Wh-" Molly starts, her jaw dropping and her voice going down to a whisper. "What the hell are you-"

A moment later, the door clicks open, and I glance at Molly. "Someone left it unlocked," I lie with a smile.

"Oohhh," she says with wide eyes.

This is fun.

"But wait," she says, "there's no elevator in here, what are you doing?"

I step inside and look around for something that looks like a panel of breakers. Finding it, I look through the switches and wires for a few moments and ask over my shoulder, "What floor does Andie live on?"

"Uh, 7th."

I raise my gloved hands to one of the rows of switches, flip a few, and unhook a few wires. Without a second thought, I shut the panel and nod for Molly to follow me out the door. I quickly lock it behind us and shut it before heading for the stairs.

"What the hell was that?"

"Electronic locks and cameras should be dealt with," I say simply. "Getting into her room will be as easy as that utility room now."

She blinks in disbelief as we start climbing the stairs. "How do you…"

"I'm good at my job," I say simply. I don't want to get into the details of my skills just yet. Preferably not at all. This isn't the first time I've used this exact tactic to break into an apartment. "You'd be surprised how lax the security can be at places like this. Nobody dares break into these kinds of places, usually. They're too well policed."

That seems to satisfy her for now, but I catch her watching me suspiciously every now and then. It's a conversation we'll probably have to have eventually, as much as I hate to admit it. "You can do a character review of me later," I add on the third time I catch her glancing.

Several flights and one picked lock later, the door to Andie's room opens, and no alarms go off. Perfect.

Molly slips ahead of me and steps into the apartment. "Andie?" she ventures, a hint of desperation in her voice. She looks back at me and whispers, "Just in case." Turning back to the room, she adds, "Stella? Taylor…?"

No reply.

I close the door behind us and step inside.

It's about what you would expect from a house belonging to three rich models. Stunningly stylish, designer furniture, and the kind of aesthetics you'd expect from a professional interior designer. Hell, they probably hired one.

In general, though, things look tidy. No signs of struggle anywhere. Andie wasn't kidnapped from her home, at least, or if she was, she went willingly.

"Andie's room is over here," she says, jabbing a thumb toward one of the rooms down the hall. "I'll check it if you look around the kitchen. I'm going to grab a set of clothes while I'm here, too," she adds, looking down at her outfit."

"Are you two the same size?" I ask.

"Close enough," she says with a weary look at her

clothes. "Better than wearing the same outfit for a third day, anyway."

"Fair enough."

Molly goes into the room, leaving me to look through the kitchen. I stride through it, my eyes scanning over everything. They don't seem to do a lot of cooking. I open the fridge and see some takeout boxes from what looks like a trendy restaurant that someone probably forgot about.

There are some supplements and other vitamins filling a few other shelves, and of course, I find a few shelves of liquor. No beer, and just a few bottles of wine.

It's all the signs of some models having to police their body image, I think with a slight frown. I've been thinking more than usual about everything that must be involved in this kind of life. Molly having to mind her public image constantly and carry on a balancing act that would drive me crazy, Andie and her friends trying to keep their bodies exactly the way their sponsors want them... I can't imagine living like that. I'd just as soon bash my managers' heads together.

Well, at the end of this trail, I'll probably be bashing someone's *manager's head, at least.*

I look at a picture of all three of the girls at the beach on the fridge. Their selfie is pretty good camera work, I have to admit, even though it looks like it's just a personal photo, not something done for modeling. Picking out Andie is easy--she looks a lot like Molly, just younger, and the way she carries herself is a little different.

Maybe it's the association of her to Molly, but the idea of Eddie Arnold actually getting a hold of her makes me furious. Spoiled celebrity child or no, nobody deserves this kind of treatment.

Just then, I hear Molly from the other room. "Oh my god...!"

I head inside Andie's room to find Molly standing over a little desk, staring at a little calendar in her hands. "What is it?"

She holds the calendar up to me with wide eyes. I give it a blank look. "What about it?"

"This is Andie's," she says, looking down at the little thing, then pointing to a date on it. "Look what she has written down for Christmas Eve!"

I squint at the date. "Goldschmidt, 3:00 PM."

Molly's eyes are wide. "Exactly! She dropped me off at the hotel at 2:00 PM that day, and that was the last time I saw her!"

I nod, my brow furrowing. "So this Goldschmidt might be the most recent person to talk to her. But this isn't much of a lead, can you find anything saying who he might be?"

"We don't have to," Molly says, tossing the calendar to the table and putting her hands on her hips. "That's the bizarre part. I *know* who Gold-schmidt is, there's only one guy with that name that we know, and we've known him for a long time." She pauses for a moment, thinking.

Finally, I make a hand gesture as if to say "And…?"

She looks me in the eye, confusion and hurt written in them. "Wes, Goldschmidt is an acting agent for huge blockbusters, usually only A-list actors." She glances back down to the calendar. "Andie…Andie must have been auditioning behind my back!"

"I'm gonna kill her, Wes," I hiss through gritted teeth.

"What's the big deal? You're a family of entertainers, aren't you? It makes sense that your little sister would be trying out for parts and stuff," he replies, shrugging behind the steering wheel. He glances over at me and I glare at him.

"You don't understand," I shoot back, shaking my head. "Andie is… vulnerable. She's smart, but too optimistic. She only sees the good in everyone and she doesn't plan things very well. I mean, she's only eighteen. She can't be expected to make good life choices at that age."

Wes snorts and I look at him angrily. "What was that for?" I snap.

"Nothing. Just the fact that you're a massive hypocrite. That's all," he replies smoothly.

I can feel my rage reaching a boiling point inside me.

"A hypocrite? How dare you? I'm just trying to look out for my sister, who just happens to be my best friend and the most important person in my life," I retort.

"Weren't you acting in big movies at her age?" Wes points out, unaffected by my anger, which only serves to make me even angrier.

"Yeah," I answer, folding my arms over my chest. "So fucking what?"

"If you could do it, why can't she?" he asks, looking at me sidelong.

I sigh. "Because I know what kind of effect that shit can have on your life. I remember what it felt like, being so young and away from home, cutting business deals, being under much more intense scrutiny than I was used to-- and that's saying a lot considering the last name I grew up with. The thing is, the reason I don't want her to do this is because *I* did it. I lived that life. And yes, it did go fairly smoothly for a while. But only because I got super lucky, and because I am a paranoid, perfectionist person who looks after herself. It was only when I got complacent and too trusting that Eddie was able to swoop in and screw things up for me," I explain. "And you don't know Andie. She's not like me. She doesn't question everything like I do. She doesn't plan for the worst. She hopes for the best and leaves it at that. And in this industry, that's a liability. A handicap. *That* is why this pisses me off so much. I'm scared for her."

"It's not your place to decide for her, though," Wes says, his voice softer and more patient this time. "Like you said, she is eighteen. It's her life, Molly. If you don't let her make mistakes on her own, she will never learn from them."

"I get that reasoning. I really do. And trust me, if she really, really wanted to do this, I would support her. As long as she was careful. But the fact that she decided to go for an audition right now, while I'm caught up in this awful bullshit with Eddie-- that tells me she's not being careful at all. She's just free-falling," I lament, tears burning in my eyes. "And nobody is there to catch her."

Wes reaches across the console to take my hand and give it a squeeze. "We are going to catch her. Okay? You may be my client, but Andie is your family, and I am not about to let this slide. We'll find her. I swear."

I raise his hand to my lips and kiss it softly. "Okay. Thank you," I answer quietly.

The whole ride to Goldschmidt's office complex, I fiddle with the burner phone. Every time I open the screen and see it still blank, the little text message icon empty, my heart sinks a little further. I wish I could just hear from her. Something. Anything. Just one word to tell me she's okay or at least alive. I know I shouldn't jump to any horrible conclusions, but I just can't help but feel like something is seriously wrong.

"You holding up okay there?" Wes asks.

I nod and wipe my eyes, mad at myself for getting all weepy. I need to be strong right now. Keep myself together. For Andie.

"Yeah, yeah. I'm fine. I just... can't stop thinking of the worst-case scenario," I admit, surprised at myself for opening up like this. "Ever since we were little, Andie and I were almost more like twins than just sisters. We have this connection-- I don't know if you could call it psychic or magic or whatever. But whenever one of us is upset, I swear, the other can feel it. One time, when I went to camp as a little girl, Andie had to stay home because she wasn't old enough to go yet. At camp, they had this huge pool. I was, I don't know, eight years old, maybe? It was a really hot afternoon. Over a hundred degrees, I'm sure. We were having a pool party, kids swimming around, jumping off the diving board, down the water slide. All that jazz. But I could only swim with those little floaties you wear on your arms, you know? And I'd left them back at the cabin on accident, so I was just sitting on the edge of the pool with my feet in the water.

"Well, apparently, unbeknownst to me, some of the older kids had figured out who my parents were. They were jealous, I guess, or maybe they just wanted to find someone who was different, easy to single out. You know how kids are. They're awful at that age," I add, shaking my head. Wes waits for me to go on. I take a deep breath. "So, I'm sitting on the edge of the pool just hanging out, feeling a little down that I can't swim with the rest of the kids, when suddenly these two older boys come strolling over to me in their stupid dinosaur-print swim trunks. I remember it all so vividly. They asked me if I lived in a big castle in Hollywood and I told them no, of course, I live in a house. I was so confused. Couldn't think of a single reason why these two boys would be talking to me. They weren't from my side of the camp. I'd never met them before. They just kept asking me questions about my family. How much money we had. What kind of car my dad drove. And I guess they found out just enough information about me to hate me, because then they each grabbed one of my arms, lifted me up, and tossed me into the deep end of the pool."

"Holy shit!" Wes gasps, looking at me with his blue eyes wide.

I nod. "Yeah. I sank like a stone. It was one of those Olympic-type pools. The deep end was probably ten, fifteen feet or something. There were so many kids splashing around in the water, I'm sure the lifeguard didn't see me at first. I just sank and sank and I remember thinking, at eight years old, shit. I'm gonna die."

"What happened?" he prompts me.

"Well, eventually one of the kids who tossed me in got cold feet and told the lifeguard I fell in. The lifeguard dove in after me and brought me back to the surface. He had to do CPR on me for like a full minute, apparently. When I came to, all I could think about was how badly I wanted to go home," I tell him. "That very night, my dad drove all the way out to pick me up. Andie insisted on going with him even though it was probably one in the morning when he got there. Turns out, at the exact time I fell in the pool, Andie had an epic tantrum. Screaming, crying, throwing toys around, begging my parents to let her talk to me on the phone. My parents could only calm her down by promising to call me later. When they called the camp to ask to speak with me, the counselor filled my parents in on what happened that day at the pool, and of course, that's when they decided I needed to just come home. Andie was only five at the time, so she doesn't remember it, really. But my parents have told me the story a hundred times, probably. Me, drowning in the pool, and Andie having a massive meltdown at home at the exact same time, worried about her big sister," I finish, a sentimental smile tugging at my lips.

"Damn," Wes says. "That's deep shit."

I laugh gently. "Yeah. It is. And we've always been like that, even today. And right now, I can feel it.

That uneasy feeling like something is wrong. I can't shake it," I say sadly.

"We'll find her, Molly. It'll be okay," Wes assures me, but I can't quite believe him. "I am wondering, though… would his office even be open the day after Christmas?"

"Oh yeah. I know Goldschmidt through the grapevine. I think we actually met once or twice at a wrap party. He's Jewish. He'll be open over Christmas," I explain quickly.

Soon, we pull up to the office with the name GOLDSCHMIDT emblazoned on the front in, fittingly, gold lettering. I'm out of the car and walking briskly toward the front door before the car even stops rolling. Wes hastily parks and runs after me, grabbing my arm and making me slow down. "Hey, hey," he says. "Calm down. If you go in there looking a bull seeing red, you'll tip 'em off."

"Tip them off?" I repeat, raising an eyebrow. "I don't give a fuck what these people think of me, Wes. They have my sister."

"Right, I know. But just play it cool. If they sense something is up, they'll be less likely to give us the information we need," he insists. I force myself to relax my shoulders and chill the hell out, even though what I want to do is march in, slam my fist on the counter, and demand to see my sister.

We walk through the glossy automatic glass doors and stroll up to a front desk where a secretary is quietly waiting, staring at a computer screen. She looks up at us with doe eyes and asks, "Hello, how can I help you? Do you have an appointment with Mr. Goldschmidt?"

I open my mouth to speak but can't think of a good answer. Wes steps in.

"Yes. We're his three o'clock," he says solidly.

The secretary cocks her head to one side, looking very suspicious. "His three o'clock canceled about an hour ago," she says.

"Hi," I speak up, giving her my most cover-girl smile. "My name is Molly Parker. I think my assistant must have accidentally canceled the appointment, but we're here now."

She looks back and forth between us a couple times, clearly trying to determine whether she'll be in more trouble for letting us through or for turning away a star like me. Apparently, the second option scares her more. She gives us a polite smile and stands up. "Of course. I'll take you back to his office. Follow me, please."

As we fall in step behind her, Wes and I exchange bemused expressions. This is definitely one perk of having a famous name and a famous face: I can open doors that are closed to most people. The secretary takes us back through a long corridor and then presses a buzzer outside a door with a frosted glass pane.

"Mr. Goldschmidt, there seems to have been a

miscommunication about the cancellation. Your three o'clock is here… a little early," she adds, biting her lip.

There's a pause, and then he replies through the speaker: "Send them in."

The secretary opens the door for us and then heads back toward the front desk. Wes and I step inside, close the door quickly, and then walk over to sit in the big leather chairs in front of Goldschmidt's desk. His eyes widen at the sight of me and he starts to reach for the phone, probably to call security. I have a strong feeling Wes and I look nothing like his three o'clock.

"Don't," Wes says, pointing to the phone in the agent's hand. He freezes, looking at me with worried eyes.

"Molly Parker?" he asks, obviously confused. I see him reaching slowly under his desk.

I nod. "Yes. And if you don't press that security button under your desk I will owe you a big-ass favor."

Wincing as he realizes he's been caught, Goldschmidt folds his hands together on top of his desk, leaning forward. "Fair enough. So, how can I help you?"

"Oh, like you don't know exactly why I'm here," I snap.

"Actually, I'm very surprised to see you around here… considering," he replies.

Wes steps forward. "What do you mean? Considering what?"

"Are you going to make me spell it out? I'm talking about that nasty business with Eddie Arnold. Seems strange that you would come here, of all places, in your situation."

Something cools off inside me. These aren't the words of a guilty man.

"You know about that," I murmur. He nods.

"Of course, I do. That's why you're here, isn't it?" Goldschmidt asks.

"No. I'm here about my sister, Andie. You were the last person to talk to her before she went radio-silent on me. I know you've been working with her secretly," I accuse.

He raises both eyebrows and leans back in the chair. "I respect the confidentiality of any client I may or may not be working with."

"Listen, drop the wishy-washy lawyer bullshit," Wes says forcefully.

"I'm gonna have to ask you to leave."

I stand up and put both my hands down on the desk. "Look, sir. Things are getting very tense with Eddie, and you and I both know it won't look good for you if you get involved. I could tell anyone I was here, drop your name… I know you want to keep your hands clean."

The agent glares at me for a long moment, then hangs his head and sighs. "Fine. Fine. Andie Parker reached out to me about auditioning for a part, wanted me to get her set up. I felt guilty about it, honestly, because it's the kind of part you would be great for, Molly. But with everything happening between you and Eddie right now… well, obviously you're out of bounds. And besides, Andie was so insistent. Determined. I've been working in this industry for a long time now, and I'm a pretty good judge of character. And I can tell you one thing for certain: Andie Parker feels like she has something to prove. She lives in her sister's shadow."

I feel my heart breaking. Is this… my fault?

Wes picks up the slack. "Thanks for the lecture, but we're here to ask about something else. Where did she go after your meeting with her on Christmas Eve?"

Goldschmidt looks shocked and confused. "Christmas Eve… she didn't show up for that meeting. She was never here that day."

Wes and I look at each other, totally lost.

"What do you mean? Where was she?" I demand.

Goldschmidt holds his hands up. "Hell if I know. I don't have a lowjack on her or anything. She's my client, not my dog."

"Is there anyone else who might have known about that meeting here?" Wes asks.

The agent thinks for a moment. "No. Just me and my secretary. And… well…"

"Well, what?" I prompt him impatiently.

Goldschmidt looks flighty, like he's considering just turning around and climbing out the window, he's so uncomfortable. "The only other person who has access to all our files and schedules is... well, Eddie Arnold."

"What?!" Wes and I exclaim at the same time.

The agent shrugs slowly. "I thought you knew. This company is owned by Mr. Arnold. He has copies of everything, all our paperwork."

I stare at Wes, my heart pounding away in my chest. If Eddie knew about the meeting, which just happened to be taking place the same day his men tried to kidnap me, and Andie never showed up...

Goldschmidt appears to pick up on the tension in the room and adds nervously, "I have a strong feeling that Mr. Arnold is about to found guilty of something I don't want to be associated with, isn't he?"

An idea occurs to me. "Yes. He is. But if you do me one big favor, I will *swear* under oath that you had nothing to do with this."

Clearly on the same wavelength, Wes jumps in. "Your secretary answers to you alone, right? Then have her send you Eddie Arnold's personal schedule."

"Hell no," I shout to Molly as she strides across the parking lot, already halfway to the car and a good twenty paces ahead of me, "there is no way I'm taking you in there!"

"Yes you *are*," she snaps back over her shoulder, and I catch a glimpse of the white-hot fire in her eyes. "You're my bodyguard!"

"Exactly," I say as I jog to catch up to her, walking alongside her and lowering my voice. "I'm your bodyguard, not a director telling you to jump out of a burning building. No way in hell am I about to drag Molly Parker into a firefight. You are my *client*."

She stops and whirls around to face me, and I have to admit, her expression is so furious that it stops me dead in my tracks. "Oh, is that all I am to you now?"

I'm dumbstruck. In the moment that passes

between us, Molly moves to the car and tosses me the keys before she opens the passenger-side door. "You said it yourself, Wes, Eddie wants me alive. He won't lay a finger on me until I'm falling into his hands. Besides, this is the only chance we've got at this. If you know another time we'll have all our eggs in one basket, I'm all ears."

Goddamn it. I shake my head and stride to the car, climbing in and turning the key. "Fine, but you're staying in the car once we're there."

She snorts, and I can tell that's not going to happen either.

All this was because the schedule we got from the secretary had some *very* interesting information on it. Eddie Arnold has been meeting with someone named Atlas fairly regularly for the past three weeks, and as luck would have it, he's meeting him again tonight, down by the docks. The short note in the schedule just said "Dock 16," which tells me all I need to know--he'll be somewhere in the vicinity. We will be too.

The only kink in the simple plan is that I know who Atlas is.

It's not the guy's real name. Atlas is the "business name" the leader of North Sonoran Security goes by, and he's exactly the kind of guy you'd expect to be using a codename like Atlas.

So naturally, Molly wants to go drop in on the meeting immediately.

We pull out onto the road, and as we do, I grumble under my breath, "If you were just a client, I'd be charging triple by now to put up with you."

Molly casts a glare at me, but I can see the faintest ghost of a smile on those lips as she looks back.

"So what *does* that make me?"

I raise my eyebrows. "Something else, that's for damn sure."

It's a long drive to the docks from where we are in good traffic, and LA traffic is never good, so I thank god that this meeting isn't taking place until midnight. That also gives us enough time to park far away from where we need to be so we can move in quietly.

"What happened to 'stay in the car'?" I ask as we both get out, and she gives me a flat look. I roll my eyes. "Right."

The docks are gloomy, vast, and industrial. Everything you'd expect and more. It's like a sea of large, metal shipping crates and the cranes used to move them around. Dockworkers are off for the day by now, so it's mostly security left moving around the place. Of course, I have a feeling security will "forget" to patrol Dock 16 much tonight.

It's the way these things go. Workers don't get

paid enough, so it's easy for shady characters to pay them off to look the other way.

"Are you sure you'll be able to move quietly?" I ask Molly as we start making our way into the maze of metal ahead of us.

"Better than you can in a leather jacket and boots," she quips, and I look down at my getup. As much as I hate to admit it, the clothes she borrowed from Andie's apartment are a little better suited for sneaking around than mine. Still, I shrug.

"Served me well enough so far."

"I'm amazed you can sneak up on anyone, lumbering around like you do," she says, a teasing edge to her voice that I smirk back at.

"I was about to say the same thing. You can smell that perfume from a mile away."

"Just because we're snooping doesn't mean we can't be a little put together," she says with a toss of her hair, and we have to fight the urge to laugh at each other.

It'll be a very short recon mission if we can't keep a hold of ourselves.

We get into position by the time night falls. Molly and I climb up a utility ladder and get on top of a shipping crate that overlooks a wide area that looks like it's used for foot traffic fairly regularly, and I can tell that not much sound travels outside it. It's the perfect place for a meeting like this.

Vegas doesn't have docks, but I know a good out-of-the-way, industrial meeting place when I see one.

We settle down out of sight, and we wait.

After a few minutes, I see Molly starting to look uncomfortable, and I raise an eyebrow at her. "You can have my jacket to sit on, if the metal's too uncomfortable," I whisper.

"I'm just thinking...what if they don't show?" she says. "This is the only lead we've got. If we're just sitting on our hands all night then that's another day Andie goes without help and-"

I hold up a finger at the sound of wheels in the distance, and that quiets her. We listen as the sound gets closer, and we can tell that there's more than one car heading our way. We exchange glances and get into a position we can watch from while staying out of sight.

I watch the first car pull up--a large, black SUV with tinted windows. As expected, once it comes to a stop, out steps a man that's easily my height and every bit as heavily built as me, wearing a tight black tank top and camouflage pants. Atlas was black ops, from what I've heard, and he never really lost the flair for military style.

A Porsche pulls up next, and I can see Molly bristle at the sight of it, telling me exactly who it is. A second later, the man who could only be Eddie Arnold steps out of the car.

My eyes go wide at the sight of him.

He's an older man with leathery skin who looks like he's been a sleazeball since the day he was born. Not much of a fighter, my instincts tell me, but men like that can surprise you if you underestimate them for a second. He looks agitated as he struts across the meeting space toward Atlas and the other mercenaries piling out of the car.

None of that is what makes my eyes go wide, though.

It's Eddie's face.

I recognize that face.

I turn to whisper to Molly, and my heart drops when I realize that while I was focusing on Eddie, she vanished. I look around to catch the top of her head descending the ladder silently.

What the fuck are you doing?! I want to scream. With the sounds of doors closing as my cover, I move to follow her.

I watch Molly get down to the ground silently before she heads to a hiding spot a little closer to the meeting, behind some stacked barrels. My heart is pounding. At that range, all it would take would be about ten seconds, and those mercenaries could spot her, throw her into a car, and be off with her.

I reach the ground and move up next to her. Neither of us have been noticed. I move to grab her by the arm by way of asking her what the hell was on her mind, but then I see my explanation.

She has a phone out, the camera lens facing the

meeting through a gap in the barrels, and she is filming the meeting.

Evidence.

I have to give it to her...she'd do well in my line of work.

Eddie speaks first, throwing his hands out to his sides in exasperation.

"So why the fuck do I only have one Parker, Atlas? I pay you fucks three times your going rate, and I feel like I'm getting half effort. You taking Christmas off, or what?"

Atlas's hard face goes harder. "The woman you're asking us to deal with is a high-profile celebrity, Mr. Arnold. And I don't have to tell you how much *your* legal battle with her is complicating things."

"Jesus fuck, you sound like my lawyer now, and I ain't paying you for that," Eddie fires back, waving a hand dismissively. "So what the fuck happened at the hotel? She was backed into a goddamn corner, I should be balls deep in her by now."

Molly is tense.

"You didn't inform us she would have skilled personal security," Atlas says, looking defensive. I recognize the look of a man who doesn't want to be working this job anymore. I might be able to use that to our advantage.

"Skilled per- what the fuck do you mean?" Eddie splutters.

"Your 'little prize' hired a freelancer," Atlas

growls. "I don't appreciate sending my men in without sufficient intel, especially when we're already going above and beyond what we'd ordinarily-"

"Oh cut the moralizing crap," Eddie groans. "Okay, okay, I get it, she gave you the slip. Shit happens. Whatever. Nobody's dead, so I don't care. As long as you kept it quiet, let's just forget about it."

Some of Atlas's men exchange glances. Molly's recording is still rolling.

"Let's focus on the *immediate* future, and I mean *immediate*," Eddie says, putting his hands together. "Because right now, Bitch Number Two is still at the lakehouse, and as soon as someone catches on to that, any plans for ransom go out the window, the media will be all over it like goddamn vultures."

There it is.

Molly casts me an urgent look, but she keeps quiet, stiff as a tree, and looks back to the meeting, biting her lip so hard I think she'll draw blood.

"If that happens, Mr. Arnold, I want to be very clear that our contract will end," Atlas says firmly. "Transporting one high-profile person like her is dangerous enough. You'll see us all tossed behind bars if you don't keep a clear head."

"Who the fuck do you think you are to talk to me like that?" Eddie snaps, stepping forward to Atlas, who doesn't budge. "Did you forget I'm the one paying you? Besides, there's no two kidnappings happening. Andie's secure, so as soon as you fucks get off your asses and locate Molly, she'll hand herself over so we can dump Andie and make it look like Molly just came to her senses and ran off with me."

"The more you try to juggle, the riskier it will get," Atlas says.

Eddie throws his hands up. "Well fuck me then, the sisters look alike enough that maybe I'll just satisfy myself rawing Andie 'till *she* decides to cooperate."

In the blink of an eye, I see Molly's hand dart to my side where my gun is holstered. My hand flashes out to catch her by the wrist before she can pull it out. My skin against hers makes a soft slap, and Atlas's guards turn their attention our way.

Shit.

"Boss!" one of them shouts. I know we have a matter of seconds before we have a lot of guns trained on us.

Molly reacts.

She keeps her phone in her left hand, grips my gun with her right, and pulls it out of its holster in the split-second that my attention is on the guards, and to my amazement, she stands up and trains the gun on Eddie.

"Don't shoot!" Atlas roars, holding his hand out to his guards in the same moment that I stand up with my other gun in hand, training it on Atlas.

Eddie looks stunned, staring dumbfounded at Molly.

Molly's hands are shaking, though, furious over what she heard, and in the tense seconds that follow, I worry that she might just pull the trigger on Eddie.

"You fucking monster," Molly hisses, glaring daggers at Eddie. "I used to think you were someone I could trust!"

"Well merry fucking Christmas to you too, Molly," Eddie says, a disgusting smile creeping over his face even as he puts his hands up. "That's a pretty ungrateful way to talk to someone who took care of you for so long."

"You tried to have me kidnapped!" she snaps. "You took Andie!"

"She's safe," Eddie says hurriedly, "and she's gonna stay that way, okay?"

"Fuck you," Molly says, tears in her eyes. "Give me one good reason not to kill you right now."

He raises his eyebrows. "Uhhh, you're welcome to do that, honey, but that's not gonna look great in court. Besides," he says, looking at the distance between us and them, "I know they taught you to shoot a little, but if you miss, things are gonna get ugly real fast."

"She has a camera, Eddie," Atlas speaks up, his eyes focused on the phone in Molly's hand. "That footage needs to come with us." He turns his attention to Molly. "Miss Parker, hand the phone over, and we'll negotiate about the rest."

"The hell we will!" Eddie snaps at Atlas, turning his attention to the bigger man. "You're still on my contract!"

"This is too much," Atlas growls, "I want that evidence destroyed, and I'm backing my men out, you're insane."

"Fuck that, I'll double your pay to get both these bitches back to the lakehouse and-"

Molly fires.

Eddie screams and puts a hand to his ear, half of which has been shot off, as Atlas and the guards duck down for cover.

Immediately, I grab Molly and pull her down before firing shots at the guards to keep them moving.

"Get her, you fucks!" Eddie croaks.

"Get her phone!" Atlas barks.

"Get to the car!" I shout to Molly, and the two of us take off in the opposite direction, into the maze of metal boxes.

The two of us sprint side-by-side, moving from cover to cover as fast as possible while we hear the sounds of boots on the ground behind us and one car revving up. The car must be Eddie, running off with his tail between his legs.

"There!" I hear someone shout behind us, and I

grab Molly, diving for the nearest cover before gunshots ring out over us.

Once we're behind cover, I fire back blindly a few times before noticing Molly, whose eyes are wide, my gun still in her hand.

"Are you hurt?" I ask urgently, and she shakes her head quickly.

"I-I almost killed him!"

"Pretty good shot, considering," I muse, waiting for the shots to ring out over us before firing back once more. I hold my hand out for my gun. "Do you mind?"

She nods, handing me the weapon and taking a breath, snapping herself out of it and looking around. "We're close to the car now--if we can get them off our backs, we could get to it."

She's able to get a hold of herself surprisingly fast, considering how fast things just boiled over.

"That's a big *if*," I grunt as one of the bullets ricochets off the metal we're hiding behind. "Are you sure we can't just give them the phone?"

"Hell no," she says, "I want *damning* evidence, and Eddie just gave it to us and then some. I want his ass locked away forever."

"Fair enough," I say, reloading one of my guns and firing back. It's only a matter of time before the mercenaries get us really pinned down, and then we're in serious trouble. "Any thoughts on-"

I follow Molly's gaze, and I realize that she's

looking at a small gap in two of the freight crates to our left that lead to the little opening where we left our car. I couldn't squeeze in there, but she could.

She gives me a look. I grit my teeth, but then a bullet pings off the wall to our right, and I take the keys out and hand them to her. "Do *not* get shot," I say, half-joking, but she's already started moving toward the gap. I see her start to wiggle through it faster than I thought possible, then have to tear my eyes away to fire back at the men.

"Freelancer!" I hear Atlas bark as the bullets stop, and I hold both guns at the ready. "We've got you surrounded! I don't know who the fuck you are, but you're in way over your head!"

Well, he isn't lying.

"You spared my men, so I'll cut you a deal," he calls. "Hand over the girl and that phone, and you walk away. No bullshit."

"Takes a lot of balls, going after a teenage girl like that," I mock Atlas, trying to keep him talking while Molly gets to the car. "Was it just too risky to go after the shampoo model? Or are your men specialized in combat with Instagram models?"

That's met with a spray of bullets, and I grin as I fire back over the top of the metal. Through the bullets, I hear the sound of a car engine start, which is exactly what I was hoping to cover up. As I hear the car roaring around, I take action.

I kick over a metal barrel next to me and roll it

out into the opening. That draws their fire just long enough for me to pop out of cover and fire off two rounds at the men. I hear a grunt and know that I've hit one of them--a man goes down, and Atlas and the last guard turn their attention to me as I dart out with both guns blazing, moving from one side of the opening to the other. A second man hits the ground, gun clattering to the floor, but I feel a bullet from Atlas graze my side, and I take cover again.

"You're wasting your time, working for these Hollywood brats, you know," Atlas taunts me, and I can hear the crunch of his boots moving out into the open. I saw the big guns he was toting, and I know they're pointed right at the barrel I'm crouching behind now. "Shame I didn't get a hold of you beforehand, you would have done well in NSS. Too late now."

"Too late for you," I grunt.

At that moment, my car's brights turn on, flooding the makeshift alley with light, and I come out of cover in time to see Atlas whirling around to face my car, driven by Molly, as she floors the gas pedal and accelerates forward.

Atlas raises his gun, but I fire mine, putting a bullet in his arm to keep him from shooting, moments before Molly hits him at full force. His body hits the ground after rolling over the car, and I run to his prone form and put a bullet in his head before he can move at the same time as Molly screeches to a halt.

And damn it all, I can't help but grin at the car and its driver.

Without another moment to waste, I rush to the car, sliding over the hood as Molly gets out. "You drive!" she says to me hurriedly, and I don't need any more prompting.

Nearly killing two people in one day takes a lot out of a person.

Once we're both in the car, I throw it into gear and tear off in the general direction I saw Eddie go.

"It's a long shot," I growl as Molly fumbles to get her seatbelt on, "but if I can see where that bastard left the docks, I might be able to catch up with him, even if he got a head-start." They're empty words, though--there's no way I can do anything but try to stay on that Porsche's trail.

"You don't need to," Molly says, getting a hold of herself and looking at me with wide, resolute eyes. "I know where he's going."

"You do?"

"He said Andie is at the lakehouse," Molly explains, nearly breathless. "That's a place he owns outside the city, a little retreat we all used to go sometimes when we were kids--I-I have good memories there," she trails off, and I can see tears trying to well up in her eyes again until she fights them back, and she blinks them away, looking at me.

"He's headed to her there, and I remember the way. Follow my directions."

A cocky smile comes to my face as I turn my attention back to the road. "You got it, Miss Parker."

From here on out, it's a race against time.

"Turn onto the highway," I direct Wes, leaning forward in the passenger seat of his car.

"The next exit coming up on the right?" he clarifies.

"Yes. Right there," I answer. I sit back as he makes the turn. I realize my body is totally tensed up, my jaw tight and aching. With a deep breath, I make a concentrated effort to calm down and relax my body, if not my racing mind.

"Now what?"

"Just drive for awhile. It's a long way down this highway," I tell him.

"Are you okay?" Wes asks quietly.

I can feel the undercurrent of what he's not saying. All the things he hasn't brought up. Those questions burning, crackling in the small space between us.

"I don't know," I reply, shaking my head. "No. I'm not, actually."

"You know the way, right? For sure?" he asks, looking over at me.

I give him a slow nod. "Yeah. I know it by heart. We used to go there all the time when I was a kid. Eddie's lakehouse. We spent summers laying out on the lawn, hiking in the hills, fishing off the dock. He had this little red rowboat. My sister and I used to take it out and paddle way out onto the lake, play card games on the open water, just drifting. Getting crazy-awful sunburns and then paddling home, exhausted, to eat hamburgers and hot dogs my dad and Eddie grilled on the back deck. Those are some of my happiest memories, Wes."

I look over at him, now not even trying to stop the tears prickling in my eyes and rolling down my cheeks. "How did this happen, huh? How did it come to this? How did the man I trusted, even maybe loved, as a kid... end up being such a fucking evil creep? It makes me question all those good memories I made back then. The whole time he was pretending to be my parents' best friend, my goofy uncle-- was he just planting the seeds for what he had planned later on? Was this his goal all along? To make me trust him so that I would make an easy target as an adult?"

Wes shakes his head. "I don't know, Molly. I'm so sorry."

"How dare he do this to me? To Andie? God, to my parents! We all trusted him. We all fell for it, hook, line, and sinker. He seemed so genuine, that lying bastard. Tell me, how the hell am I supposed to trust anyone now? Ever?" I cry, running my fingers back through my hair in frustration. Wes is conspicuously silent.

Which only reminds me of something Eddie said during the fight at the docks.

"Especially with you associating with that mafioso."

My stomach flip-flops. If I don't say something now, I'll regret it. I can't let this-- whatever this is-- go any further without getting some answers first.

"Go ahead," Wes says suddenly, his voice gruff. "Ask."

"How did Eddie recognize you?" I murmur, almost afraid to look at him.

There's another long, painful silence. He's mulling it over, choosing his words.

"Are you sure you want to know?" he asks. For some reason, this just pisses me off.

I round on him with a glare, my cheeks burning hot. "I asked, didn't I? Come on, Wes. It's not like I haven't had suspicions. The way you fight. The shady skills you have. The stack of burner phones. The fact that you won't tell me a damn thing about yourself and your past even though I've spilled my fucking guts to you. Who are you? *What* are you?"

Wes closes his mouth, a steely expression on his face. He's clamming up on me.

"You told me to ask, and I asked. Now you have to tell me," I demand.

"I take it back. We're not talking about that shit," he says, a warning note in his voice. But I don't care. I'm not just going to drop it. Not now.

"No. You don't get to go back on your word," I tell him, shaking my finger at him angrily. He glances over at me with those beautiful blue eyes flashing, but I won't back down.

"Now is not the time, Molly," he says.

"Are you fucking kidding me? Everything is falling apart around me. Everyone is lying to me, sneaking around, doing shit behind my back. I'm relying on you, Wes. Right now, you are all I have. Can I trust you or not? I'm so fucking tired of being lied to. Give me the truth now or stop the car and let me walk the rest of the way!" I shout, my voice cracking as tears pulse down my cheeks. Wes heaves a sigh, shaking his head. I can tell I've struck a nerve. Good.

I put my hand on the door handle, a warning sign to him that I mean it.

He clicks the door lock.

"You want the truth?" he asks in a low, dark voice.

"Yes! That's what I want, Wes. I want you to tell me who the hell you are."

"Fine. You really want to know? Okay! I'm Wes Jameson, former mafia grunt worker. I'm from Las Vegas, Nevada and I've been running away from that place for years, afraid to look back and see it following me. When I was a kid, I lived with my mom. She was a single mom, working her damn ass off to make ends meet. Vegas isn't cheap. She was a blackjack dealer at a casino, working all hours of the night to put food on the table and clothes on my back. She's a fucking superhero to work as hard as she did. She was exhausted all the time. Never took a sick day or a vacation. When I got a little older, I got so tired of watching my mom run herself ragged. I worked odd jobs, trying to help out after school and on weekends, but it never made much of a difference. We were dirt-poor, living on the outskirts of town, surrounded by all those neon lights and the glamor and money of Vegas life without being able to even touch it ourselves. So, yeah. The mafia recruited me. Offered me a life I'd only dreamed of. Money, notoriety, women, fast cars-- the world I'd stood on the outside of for my whole life. And you know, Molly? For years, it was fucking awesome. They gave me easy jobs. Drive this car. Stand guard at that door. Follow that mark. Until that wasn't enough for them.

"That's how they get you. Hook you in with

promises of easy, fast money, and then they escalate it. Give you harder work. Dark work. Things nobody should be doing, especially a dumbass kid like I was. They made rob stores, stalk people. Send threats. Did I want to do any of that? No, of course I fucking didn't. But I had no choice. It's not like a regular job. You can't just put in your two weeks' notice and leave with a letter of recommendation. If they say jump, you say how high. And then they bumped it up too far. They ordered me to kill this guy, this poor alcoholic gambler who was a regular at my mom's casino. He owed the mafia big money, and they found out he was planning to skip town. So they demanded that I lure the guy out to the desert and kill him."

"Jesus," I swear. "What did you do, Wes?"

"I got out. They were threatening to kill my mother, Molly. The most important person in my whole world. The reason I got involved with the mafia in the first place. So, I ran. I ran away to Los Angeles and started over, doing the only barely-marketable skill I learned with the mafia: using my physical strength to protect some people and threaten others. I've tried to bury where I came from, who I used to be. But that's how I know who Eddie is, and that's why he knows me. We come from the same dark place. His real name is Eduardo Abruzzi, and he's been in the area for a long time. He was sent here as an emissary to recruit and stake a claim for this one-deadly crime family from New York," he says.

"*Once*-deadly?" I ask.

"Yes. The organization has more or less collapsed by now, but Eddie is resourceful. Versatile. The family didn't know what they had in him. Underestimated his ability to blend in and make do with the cards he's been dealt. He made a new life for himself out here," he says, "and I guess he got lucky. Fell in with the right people. Smooth-talked his way to the top. Met people like your parents, and gained their trust."

My mind is racing. It seems so fucking crazy. Eddie... a secret mafioso?

But then, certain memories come floating back to me. Times when he would disappear for weeks at a time on some mysterious business trip, always returning with lots of cash to spend. Conversations he would sneak out to his car to have. Hush-hush discussions with sketchy-looking guys who would come to the lakehouse out of nowhere.

It was there in front of me all along. Eddie Arnold... actually Eduardo Abruzzi.

"He was lying to us all along," I mumble. Then, an even more horrible thought occurs to me. "Or maybe he wasn't. What if-- what if my parents knew?"

Wes shakes his head. "No, Molly. I'm sure they had no idea. Guys like Eddie survive by keeping that shit under wraps. He wouldn't have ever shown that side of him to people like your parents. He needed them to believe he was squeaky-clean. It helps his image to have folks like that on his side. Potential alibis. Character witnesses. No, he was living a double life, like so many of them do."

"And what about you, Wes?" I ask, my voice trembling.

"Where do I turn?" he asks, ignoring my question.

I glance out the window, wracking my brain for the right instructions. I recognize a field from my childhood. We're getting close. "Turn up at that next street. To the right. It's in the woods, further in."

Wes is quiet as we turn down the little country road, the rarely-maintained road rough and uneasy. The car shakes and grumbles over the gravel. I'm still staring at the side of Wes's face, waiting for him to answer me. I'm not going to just let this go. I need to know the truth.

"Wes," I say, prompting him.

He ignores me, staring straight ahead. My heart sinks.

"Wes!" I cry out. "Answer me. Please!"

"What? What do you want to know, Molly? I've already told you everything. What else is there? You got my pathetic, tragic life story. What more could you possibly want? I don't tell anyone this shit, you know? Nobody knows who I am. Where I come from," he shoots back, those eyes blazing with a fiery rage. And something else. Sadness, maybe. Regret.

"I want to know if you're still in that life," I ask, enunciating every word. "I want to know if the guy I've been hiding out with, the man I've been fucking, is someone I should be afraid of. I want to know if I've been sleeping with the enemy."

"I'm a bodyguard, Molly. That's why I'm here right now."

"That's not what I'm asking."

"My friend Cody got me started. Hooked me up with the protection agency your stuffy-ass lawyer hired me from. I'm doing my job," he says firmly.

"This? This is *just* your job? You said it yourself, this is more than that," I say.

"Fine. You want me to spill that part of my soul, too? I feel-- *something* for you, Molly. I don't know why I can't just treat you like any other client. I don't know why I'm going out on a limb for you and your family. I don't have the answer. I've worked with beautiful women before. I've had assignments that felt too personal. But nothing like this. Nobody like you," Wes fires back at me, gritting his teeth.

"Then tell me the truth," I plead. "If you feel something for me the way I feel something for you, then be honest. Give me the ending of that story, Wes. That man the mafia made you lure out to the desert. Did you kill him? Did you kill that guy, Wes?"

The car rolls to a stop. Wes, still silent, points

straight ahead. I tear my eyes away from him and look out in front of us. The lakehouse sits in the near distance, shielded partially by beautiful, slightly overgrown flowering hedges.

"We're here," Wes says.

"This is it," Molly says, her voice thick with more emotions than I could know what to do with. "This is the lakehouse up ahead."

We're coming up to a small road that leads to a lakehouse that's only modest by LA standards. It's still clearly a vacation home close to home--spacious and modern, minus the addition of an old-fashioned dock and wooden shed.

And Eddie's car is parked outside it already.

I turn the lights off as we turn onto the road.

"He beat us here," I say in a low growl. "He's probably ready for us."

"I swear to god," Molly says through gritted teeth, leaning forward against the dashboard, "if he hurt one hair on Andie's head, I'll kill him." Her voice tells me she means it, and I don't blame her.

"I would bet she's relatively safe," I say. "If Eddie

has any idea what he's doing--and I think he does, to some extent--he won't have done anything to her. I think he still has some twisted idea in his mind of you two being together, and he'll do anything it takes to make you cooperate." I hold back from saying that he probably won't kill Andie for that reason, because the last thing Molly needs right now is a mental image of that happening.

"Okay, so, crazy aging agent is holed up inside the house with my sister, he's probably armed, and he's definitely expecting us. Got a plan?"

"You know this place better than I do," I say as I bring the car to a stop by a small tree, looking to Molly. "What's the layout?"

Molly bites her lip, thinking a few moments. "Okay, there are two big windows in the living room, so we shouldn't go in through the front--he'd see us immediately. The kitchen door is loud, unless he's had it replaced, so that's no good." She clenches her eyes shut, thinking hard. "I remember a window in the bedroom. I wasn't allowed to go in there, so I tried to catch a peek as much as I could."

"Obviously," I say.

She smiles. "I think that might be our only way in."

"It's big, but there are only so many ways to get into a house where someone's expecting you and we don't have the benefit of noise to cover us," I say, loading my guns and making sure I'm ready for a fight. Before I strap them onto me, I pause, then hand one of the guns to Molly. She takes it and nods resolutely.

"I don't know what we're going to be going in for, but I know I couldn't keep you back here if I tried," I say with a lopsided smile. "So I won't."

"You learn fast," she says with a wink. I put my hand on the door handle, but she stops me with a hand on my shoulder. "Hey, Wes?"

I raise my eyebrow. She hesitates.

"I...I know things got a little tense on the way here, but...I'm glad I hired you."

My turn to wink. "I'm still on the clock, sweetheart."

We get out of the car and make our way toward the house.

After what feels like an eternity, we come up to the docks, moving as quietly as possible. Along the way, we pass the little shed, its door hanging open and creaking in the breeze.

I exchange a glance with Molly, then move toward it, gun raised. I stick my head in.

Nothing.

There are a few big plastic kayak paddles hanging up, along with a few pieces of boating equipment and lifejackets that haven't been touched in ages. I notice Molly staring at them a while, and it hits me that these are parts of her childhood we're looking through, now untouched and covered with grime from the years.

It must be hard to see, on top of everything else.

I nod for her to follow me, and she gets a hold of herself and gets moving.

There are no lights on inside. I don't like that. We stalk around to the side of the house, Molly leading me to the bedroom she was talking about. Indeed, there's a window just big enough for me to get into.

While I'm looking at the window lock, I see Molly put a hand to her mouth, and I quirk an eyebrow at her. She points inside the house.

It's hard to see inside, because the only natural light is the sliver of the moon above, but it's just enough to be able to see what's clearly a small woman's figure in the room.

She's sitting down in what looks like a chair, in total darkness, and I don't need good lighting to tell that she's tied up.

That's Andie.

I watch intensely for a few moments and see that her chest is rising and falling--she's alive. I reach over and give Molly's hand a squeeze, and she squeezes back. Hard.

I tug her downward, and we crouch low to the ground so that I can whisper to her. "I go in first. You after."

She nods.

I stand up and carefully remove the window

screen. Houses are a different beast to break into, compared to apartments, but it's nothing I can't handle. Silent as I can be, once the screen is off, I start working on the window, gently pushing the frame back and forth until the motion pushes the simple hinge-lock open.

Eddie clearly keeps his windows oiled, which works to our advantage. Old and rusty windows creak like the devil when broken into.

It couldn't be more silent as I slide the window open. I see Andie's figure tense up, but she doesn't move a muscle. She knows I'm here, but she's smart enough not to make noise. That must mean that Eddie's in the house, waiting for us.

I haul myself up and crawl into the window, and just like that, I'm inside the house.

Once inside, my eyes adjust, and I can see that Andie is gagged, too, her bindings tied to the bed. She looks terrified, a blindfold stained with tears as she sits there, nearly shivering with fear.

I'm going to make Eddie pay for this.

I take a step forward, and as soon as I do, a voice to my right makes my hairs stand on end.

"Gun down. Hands up."

Fucking hell.

I freeze. Slowly, I start to turn my head to the closet, but Eddie saves me the effort by stepping forward, and the gleam of his pistol catches the faint moonlight just enough to tell me what it is.

"Did I fucking stutter?" Eddie snarls, holding his pistol with both hands, training it on my head. "Gun. Down."

My face twists into a grimace, but I slowly hold my gun out and lower it to the ground, then stand back up, putting my hands behind my head.

"That's more like it," Eddie says, kicking the gun toward the wall.

I hear a sob come from the chair, and I look over to see Andie shaking, fresh tears streaming down her face. She must have heard Eddie come in to lay his trap and been helpless to stop it the whole time-- she'd have been killed if she said anything.

But my thoughts are on Molly, heart pounding.

I can't show any sign of worry now, though.

"Into the living room," Eddie orders, "*now.*"

"You got it, Eddie," I say. "You're the boss."

"Don't fucking condescend me you piece of shit," he barks, and he kicks the back of my knee, making me grunt as I nearly fall down, but I start moving down the hall.

I have to be careful here. My own life is at risk, sure, but one poorly aimed bullet could mean Andie or Molly could get hurt. I won't risk that for anything.

I'm marched into the spacious living room, a big place with large couches, a massive television, and a coffee table.

"Cozy place," I say dryly.

"Yeah, real fuckin' lap of luxury," Eddie growls. "On your knees."

I obey, but I need to keep Eddie talking. "You're really going to do this?" I say as I kneel down, hands still on my head. I hear Eddie approach me from behind, and I know there's a finger on his trigger, about a millimeter away from ending my life.

"I don't know where Molly found you," he says, "but you're more trouble than you're worth. Because of you, everything is fucked. Don't even *try* to bargain. Face it, kid, you just picked a bad job for the wrong actress."

"No bargains," I say, keeping my voice calm. "You and Molly go hand-in-hand here, I know that," I lie. "And things are messy enough as it is, you said so yourself. Think hard, Eddie: do you *really* want to have to deal with a body if you're about to get Molly to come back to you?"

"Nice try, kid, but that won't matter," Eddie says with a chuckle. "I'm already way ahead of you." There's an edge to his voice that tells me he's off the deep end. Maybe he's tweaked-out on something, but he's jumpy and liable to do anything. But I have to keep him talking. Every second bought counts.

"How do you figure? The way I see it, you could skip town right now and nobody would know where you went. Guy like you must have friends in high places." I don't let it slip that I know those *friends* are crime lords in New York--that would make me a loose end. "Things don't look good right now, Eddie, you could start over somewhere fresh real easy."

"Sure will--once I have Molly," he says in a gravelly voice. "You think I haven't thought on my feet before? I put a bullet in your head, then one in Andie's, set the place up to make it look like you kidnapped her for ransom and the two of you killed each other in a struggle."

My gut wrenches. This guy has no conscience.

"Then," he continues, "I get some guys with more stones than NSS to grab Molly, and the two of us fly home to Italy where I've got some family that will treat us right, make her warm up to me while straddling my-"

CRACK.

I whirl around to the sight of Eddie staggering down before Molly, who just whacked him over the head with a red paddle from the shed out back, *hard*.

I take my chance and lunge at Eddie, bowling him over and pinning him to the ground. He grunts as his back hits the floor, and I punch him across the face, sending teeth flying onto the carpet. He brings a knee up to try and strike me in the balls, but I wrench him to the side.

He struggles in my grasp, but not against me--I realize he's going for the gun he dropped when Molly hit him.

His fingers brush against the handle, and the

paddle comes down hard on his hand, and this time, I hear the crack of breaking bones.

He shrieks in agony, and I lunge forward to grab the gun. The next second, I put it against the back of Eddie's head as he groans in pain under my weight.

"Fucking son of a bitch," Molly snarls at him. A moment later, I see a freed Andie appear behind her with a face as white as a ghost.

I pause with my gun to Eddie's head, the pathetic worm of a man breathing heavily under me, glaring up at Molly with pure hatred.

"You seething, ungrateful bitch," he croaks. "I could have given you everything, but you'll always just be a spoiled fucking brat." He tries to struggle under me. "Go ahead, pull the trigger you piece of shit!"

I cock the gun, my face locked in a scowl.

Once again, I have someone's defenseless life in my hands.

My finger on the trigger.

MOLLY

"Remember how it used to feel here?" Andie asks me quietly. We're standing at the end of the wooden dock, watching the sun just barely beginning to rise over the horizon. The sky is gray and purple, a dusty pink starting to stain the clouds crowning the sun. The water is still, only the faintest ripples breaking the surface. I give Andie's hand a little squeeze, looking over at her. She looks dog-tired, with dark bags under her eyes, her cheeks pale and drawn.

"Yeah. It used to feel like freedom. Like endless summer," I reply. "It's hard to believe how safe we used to think we were. This place was like our home away from home, wasn't it?"

"I swear, if I close my eyes, I can still smell Dad grilling hotdogs and hamburgers on the back deck up there. Mom pouring glasses of champagne. She used to get so tipsy on those summer nights," Andie giggles. "I remember when I was little I just thought she was more fun."

"She *was* more fun. I mean, she's never boring, but with a glass of champagne you can even convince her to dance," I add, grinning at the memory of our beautiful, famous, well-respected mother Pamela Parker spinning and whirling around in the yard with a champagne flute raised high in her hand. We were all so carefree on those summer days and nights, far enough away from the city to escape the probing eyes and camera flashes of the paparazzi. Here at the lakehouse, we all let our hair down and relaxed.

"Remember when we dragged that beat-up, old boombox out here and all danced to that Britney Spears CD you and I bought with our allowance?" she laughs.

"Yes! How could I forget? Dad and Uncle Eddie were so--" I stop short, realizing what I just said. My heart sinks. Andie steps closer and gives me a one-armed hug of reassurance.

"It's okay," she says. "We're just gonna have to rearrange our memories a little bit. Maybe there was a bad guy waiting around, taking up space in our best memories, but he's only a tiny part of it. All those good times... it wasn't just him. It was all of us. You, me, Dad, and Mom. And Britney Spears," she adds, smiling.

We hear the thud of heavy footsteps behind us and we turn around to see Wes walking up to us, side by side with a police officer holding a notepad and pen. I've already been questioned for several hours since the cops first turned up at the lakehouse, but I'm sure they're nowhere near finished with me. A high-profile case like this, with people like my sister and I and well-known Hollywood agent Eddie Arnold involved, the police need as much information as possible to keep things carefully under wraps. The police, as well as my family, will be under intense scrutiny, I'm sure.

Just as I'm starting to feel a little anxious, Wes gives me a smile, which makes my heart skip a beat. I feel warm from my head to my toes, just from that one look.

"Sorry to interrupt, ma'am, but I need to take down a statement from Miss Parker," the cop says. Then he blushes. "Oh. You're both Miss Parker. I need to speak with Andie Parker first," he clarifies bashfully.

"Okay, what do you need to know?" Andie asks him, already going into business mode. The whimsical look leaves her face and she furrow her brow, nodding intently as the cop explains what he needs from her. As he drones on and on, she seems to realize that this is not the best place for the conversation.

Andie glances between Wes and me, then interrupts the cop, saying, "Excuse me, sorry, but could we go sit down on the deck to talk? I'm still really exhausted."

"Oh-- oh, of course," the policeman agrees. As they turn to walk away, he adds over his shoulder, "Miss Parker-- Molly-- will you be available for some routine questioning over the next few days? I know one of my officers spoke to you earlier, but there will some other details to fill in."

"Yes. Should I come to the station tomorrow?" I ask him.

He grins. "That would be great. And, uh, pardon me if this is inappropriate, but my daughter loved you in *The World Enders*. Do you think I could get her an autograph from you tomorrow, as well? I totally understand if you'd rather not--"

"That's perfectly fine," I interrupt, laughing. "In fact, if you'd like to bring her in to the station, perhaps she might like to meet me herself in person?"

The cop's face lights up. "Oh, she would love that! Thank you!"

"Looking forward to it," I tell him, smiling.

Andie pokes her tongue out at me from behind the cop and I have to bite my lip to stop from laughing. The cop and my sister walk off to the deck for further questioning, leaving Wes and me alone on the dock.

He puts an arm around my shoulders. "How are you feeling?" he asks genuinely.

I shrug and give him a noncommittal, "Eh."

He laughs. "Just a day in the life, huh?"

I lean my head on his shoulder. "No. Not at all, actually. This is the most excitement I've had for a very long time. Maybe ever. And I would be very happy to go the rest of my life without another day of this kind of excitement."

"What kind of excitement would you prefer?" he asks pointedly. I elbow him gently in the ribs and give him a grin, rolling my eyes.

"You're gross," I laugh.

"Yeah, probably," he agrees jokingly. "Want to see something that will make you feel a whole lot better?"

I raise an eyebrow. "Uh, sure?"

He takes me by the hand and leads me around to the front of the lakehouse, where several cop cars are parked at odd angles, having all arrived in a huge rush. I would be lying if I said I didn't think part of their hurry was just some secret interest in seeing Andie and I. Catching the big scandalous news before anyone else. But either way, whether for genuine or selfish reasons, it was nice to have them arrive on-site so quickly. Especially considering how far out of the way this lakehouse is. Now that I'm older and I know more about the kind of man Eddie was all along, I understand another purpose for his owning this place. It's the perfect location to lay low and work under the radar. Away from prying eyes. Out here in the woods without a neighbor for miles. I shudder to think what kinds of dark, underground business went on here.

It's so strange to think that this place can hold so many sweet memories for me and still have belonged to the likes of Eduardo Abruzzi. This lakehouse has seen so many bizarre things.

"Look over there," Wes says, pointing to a car further up the long drive way.

Three cops have Eddie in handcuffs and are dragging his sorry ass over the gravel to force him into the back of the squad car. He's fighting every inch of the way, yelling about how his lawyers will sue every one of their sorry asses.

"You can't do this to me! You'll never pin me down! I'll see all you fuckers in court! You bastards have no fucking clue who the hell you're dealing with!" Eddie is raging, kicking his legs like a small child having a tantrum. It's an almost comical sight-- the man who's been terrorizing me and making my life hell, reduced to a whiny, self-important caricature of himself.

"You're right," I say.

"About what?" Wes asks.

"Seeing that *does* make me feel a lot better," I explain, smirking.

"Good. I hope that bastard gets locked away

forever. I don't want him or anyone else to fuck with you and your family ever again. But if they do… well, you know how to find me," Wes says. And something about the wording of his statement makes me sad. My heart aches, urging me to say something, do something, stop this train before it leaves the station without me.

What is it? What is my heart trying to tell me?

I so rarely listen to what my heart has to say.

Before I can dig around for the words, another police officer walks up to us.

"Ma'am, it's nearly morning. Would you like a ride home?" the cop asks.

"Oh, no thank you. I'm already going to be swarmed by the paparazzi. The last thing I need is a police escort to draw more attention," I tell him, smiling. "But thanks for the offer."

The cop nods politely and walks back over to his squad car.

"So, how is it that you're planning to get home?" Wes asks emphatically.

I look up at him and shrug. "I could call my parents. Or a taxi."

"Hmm. That you could," he agrees coolly.

Why are we playing this stupid game?

"I should wait for Andie, maybe," I muse aloud. "I'm sure she doesn't want to be left here all alone. Probably."

"Makes sense," Wes agrees. He's keeping his tone

even, unaffected. Like he's just as afraid as I am to say the wrong thing, scare me away, imply something that would forever alter the dynamic between us.

And what dynamic is that, anyway?

"I suppose my contract to you is finished," he adds, putting his hands in his pockets. "Your lawyer hired me to look after you and guard you from Eddie Arnold. Well, Eddie's in custody and he's not going to be a threat to anyone anytime soon."

My heart is breaking and I have no way of pushing the two halves back together. I simply nod. "Yeah. I guess that's true. You already went way above and beyond what your job required of you, too. I-I'll definitely give you a great review, if that's… a thing," I tell him lamely.

Wes and I stare at each other for a moment, soaking in the tension. That electricity between us is snapping, crackling, threatening to burn us both alive if we don't do something. say something. Bridge the gap or break it, but don't leave it hanging like it is. I get the sense that we're both dangling over the edge of a sheer cliff. The big fall.

"I could drive you home," Wes offers softly. "I don't want to just leave you here."

"But your job is done," I tell him, wondering why the hell I'm saying this. What am I doing? Why am I pushing him away the same way I push everyone away? Is he really just like all the others who have tried to get close to me? Is he not completely different? Something new and exciting and maybe a little bit scary, but beautiful?

Wes reaches out and takes both my hands in his.

"This isn't part of my job. It's... a favor," he explains, shrugging.

"Okay," I accept. We say goodbye to Andie, who tells me she's fine catching a ride home from the police. Then Wes and I climb into his dark sedan and pull out of the driveway, starting the long stretch back to the big city, where maybe we'll part ways and never see each other again. The thought makes me more than sad-- it makes me ill. Like I'm considering chopping off my arm or cutting out my heart. Do I need it anymore? Do I want it?

What do I have to lose except this hammering heart and the warmth he emanates? The safety I feel when he's nearby? The calm that passes over me when I gaze into those radiant blue eyes? How can I just toss it all aside and go back to my former life alone?

As we roll down the woodsy gravel road, I turn to look at him. His face is stony, his expression blank, but I can see his jaw tightening. He's tense, too. Waiting for something. A sign, maybe? For me to make the first move?

Am I brave enough to make that leap?

"Wes, you never told me the answer to the question I asked before," I say suddenly, surprising myself as the words tumble out into the air.

He nods. He already knows the question.

"His name was Joe Mackey. They told me to kill him or they'd kill my mother. They could've chosen anyone else to do the job, but they picked me. They wanted to make an example of me, show their clout. They could force me to do whatever they wanted, and with blood on my hands, I would be even more wrapped up in the mafia. They would have black-mail. Something to hold over me, to make it so I could never defy them. They would have total control over me, use me like a puppet. And I did lure Mackey out into the desert. I told him I would help him escape to Mexico, get as far from the mob as he could.

"He showed up, and I was nervous. I knew if this didn't go the way I planned, my mother's life would be void. So I did what I had to do. I took his jacket and shot a bullet through its chest. Spilled pig's blood from the butcher all over the scene. I left it right there on the sand, where I knew the boss would find it. I gave Mackey a new forged passport, a bus ticket, and some money. I told him to get the hell out of dodge, and if he ever dared to show his face in Vegas again, I would *really* kill him. I hopped in the car, drove him to the bus station, watched him board the bus, and then I took a small bag of important things I owned and I drove to Los Angeles without stopping. I never looked back. It was a long time before I worked up the courage to reach out to my mother. I was afraid that the mafia was still watching me, watching her. I was worried that I would put her in more danger. But I needed to know if she was okay. So I began sending letters, signed with a fake name. At first, she kept asking who I was, what I knew about her son who disappeared. But after awhile, she recognized my handwriting, my turns of phrase. She knew me better than anyone. So that's how I kept in touch with her. I explained in as vague detail as I could, what happened, and why I had to ditch town.

"Ever since then, I've been running, Molly. Hiding from my past. From who I was. I think once the mafia realized that I did their bidding and left, they determined it was okay to let me go. The Vegas boss is sadistic. He was more interested in forcing me to perform some horrific, evil act than actually keeping me around. I went so far off their radar, they just moved on. In Vegas, there is an endless supply of young men itching for fast money and a dangerous life. They replaced me. That was never the life for me. But it is a part of me. I'm sorry for never showing you who I truly was, Molly. You of all people deserve to surround yourself with people you can trust. I'm sorry to have betrayed that trust," Wes finishes, his voice morose and regretful.

It takes me a moment to process everything he's said.

Now you know, my heart whispers. *You know the truth. How do you feel?*

I know the answer. I feel the same.

I reach over to take his hand. Wes glances over at me, surprised. I give him a wide grin and tell him, "Thank you for telling me. And don't apologize. I've known exactly who you are all along. My heart recognized yours from the start, Wes. You may have been hiding from your past, but I could see the true you. I'd know if you were faking-- I'm an actress. That's my whole job. And that guilt you're carrying? You need to let it go. You saved my life. You saved my sister's life. As far as I'm concerned, you're a fucking hero, Wes Jameson. And apart from that... I like you. A lot. More than I ever thought I could like someone."

"Molly," he says gently, still in shock.

"Let me finish. It's my turn to talk now," I tell him. "I know you're doing your job. I know you're a busy guy with your own life. I know I'm not the kind of girl you usually like. Our lives are so different. I'm stubborn and ambitious and a workaholic. But you know what? So are you. And when I'm with you, all that noise and static in my head just goes away. You make me feel warm, and safe, and happy. I know this probably sounds crazy, but Wes, I think I'm falling for you. And whatever you choose to do with that information, I'll accept. But if you're going to tell me your truth, then it's only fair that I give you mine, too. So there it is."

Wes is silent at first, and my heart starts to sink. Still, I refuse to regret laying everything out on the table. I need to be honest about my feelings for once, instead of just burying them under piles of work and promises that maybe later I'll let my heart speak. This time, I'm going to follow it. As the car bumps off the gravel road and onto the highway, he turns to me with a bright smile and his blue eyes blazing.

"Well, damn," he says, laughing. "Here's a little more truth for you: I like you, too. Hell, after seeing the way you handled yourself last night… I might even love you."

The word stings through my heart like an arrow. I can see him swallow hard, like it was difficult for him to admit. He said the words like it was a joke, but I know. He means it. I felt it long before he gave breath to the statement. I can't help but smile.

"You know, I might just love you, too," I confess, laughing.

I smile down at the headline and short article on the tablet Cody is holding up for me, shaking my head in disbelief.

PRINCESS AND THE PAUPER: WEDDING IN PALM-TREE PARADISE!

I was glad to find out that Molly gets as much a kick out of the tabloids as I do--especially when she's the one who leaked the headline.

About a week ago, in the middle of all our plans, Molly and I cooked up this grand idea about a star-studded wedding in Maui, at this really nice spot where her parents got married, the kind of place that paparazzi would eat up if they got wind of it. And that's exactly the kind of wedding we leaked to the press.

Misleading the cameras so theatrically makes it all the sweeter when Cody lowers the tablet, and I look over to my new wife with a stupid grin on my face. Molly's laughing into her hand, nearly spilling her second glass of champagne, her bridal dress looking absolutely stunning in the sunlight that shines down on Joshua Tree National Park.

Our *real* wedding ceremony has just ended, and the reception is underway--if you can call it that.

"They're gonna be *pissed* when they catch on," Cody says to Molly with a wicked grin.

"Let 'em be," she says, waving her hand. "Wedding's already over, they missed their million-dollar shots."

The grand Maui wedding was just a front for our quiet, peaceful ceremony in the middle of the woods with only our closest friends and family. The little clearing we rented is perfect--tall trees surround us to give us a nice, rustic space that's lightly decorated with lights strung up among some of the trees. There was a carpet laid out for the ceremony, and that's still getting trampled now that the reception has started in the same little clearing.

We may have been economical with space, but we spared no expense for the quality of the food. I didn't even realize champagne was only technically real champagne if it comes from the part of France with that name--and I never thought I'd taste the stuff, either, but it's damn good. The chefs that catered the reception are some of the best LA has to offer, and the food comes from around the world. I'm surprised the aroma wafting through the woods doesn't draw half the state's bear population.

Cody winks at us and heads off to mingle with the other guests when he sees my mother rushing up to us.

"My boy is married!" Wanda gushes as she throws her arms around me, and I laugh, winking at Molly over Wanda's shoulder as she tries to squeeze the life out of me. "Wes, I'm so proud of you!"

"Thanks, Mom," I say as she lets go, grinning down at her. "Can't tell you how glad I am you were able to make it down here."

"Oh hush, I wouldn't miss it for the world!" she says, turning to Molly and wrapping her in a tight hug too. My turn to snicker at Molly over Wanda's shoulder as she nearly goes purple in the face.

I know that's an exaggeration--the casino usually works Wanda too hard to ever take a break, but we made sure she was compensated for her time off.

"Great to have you, Ms. Jameson," Molly squeaks. The two have had a chance to meet, of course, and it was nice to see that they actually got along pretty well.

Not as well as with Molly's parents, though. Wanda and Pam have been inseparable since they got in the same room together.

"And you know, that old casino might not even

be something to worry about anymore," Wanda says as she breaks away, beaming at us both. "I was just talking to Pam before the ceremony, and don'tcha know it, she wants to cast me in something she's been working on! A TV role!" Wanda raises her eyebrows and makes a can-you-believe-it! face. "Me! On TV! But it's supposed to be a secret, so don't tell her I told you."

I make the zipper gesture across my lips. "Welcome to LA, Mom."

"She gave me a heads-up," Molly says, a broad smile on her face. "You may or may not have a few apartments on a list for us to go check out for you."

"This one's on me, Mom," I say, nodding in agreement.

Wanda bites back a smile so wide it must hurt her face, and she gives me a teary hug before she waves her hands and composes herself. "Enough about that for now--I'm so happy for you two!"

"Where are you planning the honeymoon?" asks Pam as she approaches from behind Wanda, Ken close behind while Pam hugs Molly and Ken shakes my hand firmly, mouthing a silent "Welcome to the family."

"We've got a few ideas on the list," Molly says once she's exchanged very European cheek-kisses with her parents. "But I think Mexico is winning out," she says with a look to me, and I nod in agreement.

"What can I say? The desert runs in my veins," I say with a chuckle.

"Preferably the more lush parts of Mexico," Molly adds, smirking and quirking an eyebrow at me, which I flash a grin at.

"Oh, Mexico is so gorgeous," Pam gushes, "and you know, I think Andie and her friends went down there last year--where *is* Andie?"

I glance past everyone else, and my eyebrows go up at what I see across the clearing. Andie is here, but she's preoccupied with her friends, who are nudging her and gesturing to none other than Cody at the champagne table. There's a light blush on Andie's face, and she keeps shaking her head in embarrassment at her friends, all of them giggling uncontrollably.

"I think Andie's busy right now," I say with a broadening grin. Molly follows my gaze, and her eyes go wide.

"Lord help me," she says, rubbing her temple.

"Think she can handle this one on her own," I say, pulling my wife--damn, I love that word now--close to me and kissing her on the cheek.

"I suppose so," she sighs good-naturedly, smiling up at me.

"We'll leave you two alone," Wanda says, waving a hand at us and looking back to Pam and Ken before pulling them away. "Come on, there's some cake with our names on it over there."

"So, tell me about Cody…" Molly says with a hint of suspicion in her voice, and I laugh.

"He's like me, if I was the kind of guy to run off to LA to be a rock star," I say casually, and Molly looks mortified. I laugh heartily, picking her up by the hips and spinning her around before I bring her down and kiss her. "I'm kidding, I'm kidding."

I am not kidding.

"Don't give me a heart attack!" she says with a laugh, and once we've settled down, we're left standing there, smiling into each other's faces for a few moments.

"This is nice," I say with finality.

"Is it?" she says, tilting her head with a playful smile on her face. Her hair is perfectly styled so that her already big curls are perfect, like a work of art.

"Yeah. I like this a lot."

"You're such a poet," she says teasingly, and I take her chin in my thumb and forefinger, a grin on my bearded--but now trimmed--face.

"I like all this a lot too," I say in a lower tone, giving her ensemble a once-over with a hungry look in my eyes.

"You don't clean up half-bad yourself, cowboy," she says, putting her hands on my face, and we come together in a soft kiss that makes my heart soar.

I'm married to her is all that goes through my head over and over again, like fireworks in my heart. I never thought I would feel anything like this, much less feel it for a woman like Molly Parker.

But that's just it, I've come to realize, she's not "a woman like Molly Parker." She's Molly. My Molly. And I wouldn't have it any other way.

The billboard outside my office has made it a lot nicer to go to work these days.

A few seconds into the kiss, though, I become aware that things are too quiet, and I open an eye to look to my right.

I do so just in time to see all the guests watching us, having paused to enjoy our moment, and they laugh and applaud for us when they realize they've been noticed, a few of them raising champagne glasses with broad, cheerful smiles. Even I can't be angry at that, and I give them a gruff wave while Molly giggles and leans into me.

"Alright, show's over," I grunt, but at that moment, I hear the sound of Cody's damned guitar, and I realize that the guests are forming a little clearing for the first dance. Cody himself is grinning devilishly at me, confirming that this is what I think it is. Damned traitor!

But without any training, I know this is something I'm ready for.

I look down at Molly, taking her soft hand in my rough one and giving a nod to the impromptu dance floor.

"Can I have this dance, sweetheart?"

"Yeah," she says, her voice dreamy as she stares up into my eyes. "I think you can."

The two of us step out together as the orange light of the twilight casts a glow over us, and we slowly move into our dance together, right there under the stars.

A dance that will last a lifetime.

EPILOGUE - MOLLY

MY HEART IS RACING. I can feel the energy tingling from my head down to my toes. I'm waiting for my cue, poised in an athletic stance, trying to keep my face smooth and unaffected by the emotional scene my costars are acting out in front of me. There's the crack of a gun-- a sound effect. My cue. I bolt from the side of the set, running in perfect form. Once I reach the hurdle, which will be CGI-morphed into a burning car, I take a soaring leap. I land gently, bend my knees, and roll to the side before jumping up back into a fighting stance with my fists in front of me, my jaw tight and my eyes fierce.

"Cut!" cries the director. "That was fucking perfect, Molly!"

The camera crew, screenwriter, director, producer, and my fellow actors present all erupt into applause for me. It's enough to almost make me blush. Almost.

"Thanks, guys," I tell everyone, grinning as my chest heaves. My costar, a startlingly handsome man named Hayden, claps me on the shoulder as I pass by. "Great work," he says.

I give him a nod and walk off set, stretching and yawning. I've been filming since five this morning, nonstop action scenes punctuated only by a brief breakfast and a couple scenes of tense dialogue. This is the first epic action movie I've been a part of since *The World Enders*, and while I'm overjoyed to be involved with this project, it has been exhausting. My life is considerably different from how it was years ago. I'm busier now.

The producer, a short, rather manic, balding man comes skittering up to me as I walk toward the craft services table, my stomach growling. I already know what he's going to say.

"You're doing a bang-up job out there, Molly, but you know you don't *have* to do all your own stunts. You're valuable to us, babe. The last thing we want is for you to break a leg or something. Not the figurative way, of course," he says quickly.

"I know, I know," I tell him as I pick up an apple and take a big bite. "But I like to be in control of the scenes I'm in. Doing my own stunts helps me stay connected with the character."

"Okay, babe. But if you change your mind, just

you say the word, and we'll hire you a double. Alright?" he says.

"Got it," I answer absentmindedly. I'm not paying him any attention, looking at the time on my cell phone screen instead. It's very close to my most favorite time of day. The hour I look forward to most of all.

Just as I'm thinking about it, I hear, "Mommy!"

I look up, grinning, to see Wes walking over to me with our toddler daughter in his arms. She's wiggling excitedly and squirming as she reaches out to me. "Hello, my little angel," I coo as I scoop her into my arms. I lean forward to give Wes a kiss.

"How was work today?" I ask him as we walk out of the building and across the parking lot to my trailer.

"Great. We landed a new gig for the gala. The one we were angling for," he says, winking. Wes has become the owner of the security firm he used to work for when he was my bodyguard. He rarely has to get involved with the physical action of the job anymore. I know he misses it sometimes, but with Katie around, it's important that we both stay safe. For her sake. Besides, he and I still have our just-for-fun tussles every now and then. We work out together, staying in shape for our jobs. It's an amazing bonding activity, especially since once we're all hot and sweaty, we get to head off to shower together…

"Oh, that's awesome!" I exclaim. "Congratulations!"

"Yeah, the new guys are all over it," he says with a grin. "How was your day?"

I roll my eyes and sigh. "Long, long, long. These five-AM shoots are getting to be a little annoying. But the director says we'll be done with the early-morning scenes after this week. So I'll have more time to spend with you and this cute little muffin!" I add, tickling Katie. She giggles and swats at my hand.

Wes says to her, "Tell Mommy what you did at daycare today."

I give him a questioning look. "Oh god, what happened?" I ask suspiciously.

He laughs. "No, no. Something good this time."

"Oh, okay," I say, relieved. Our daughter has inherited all our most troublesome traits. She's stubborn, overly energetic, and fiercely independent. She's only three, but she's been known to backtalk her teachers already.

"I was in a movie," Katie says, grinning. She's very pleased with herself.

"A movie?" I repeat, raising my eyebrows.

"Yeah! I sang the ABCs," she explains, clapping.

"Good job!" I tell her, kissing her on the cheek. Over her shoulder, I give Wes a dubious expression. He snorts.

"They said they're making a recording of all the

kids singing songs. To send the parents at the end of the year," Wes explains. I relax a little.

"Okay. Well, that sounds fine," I confess, relieved. Katie is precocious and loves being the center of attention, so I can tell she's going to be begging me to let her join the industry in a few years. But that's a problem for the future. For now, we're keeping all that under lock and key. I want Katie to have a calm, normal childhood. Well, as normal as it can be considering how her parents are. I smile and lean over to kiss Wes again.

"Ew!" Katie cries out, burying her face in my shoulder. Wes and I laugh.

"You ready to go spend the weekend with Grandma Wanda?" I ask her. She bounces up and down on my lap, overjoyed.

"Yeah, yeah, yeah! Yay!" she bursts out, hardly able to contain herself.

We spend as much time together as a family that we can manage between our demanding careers, but sometimes Wes and I just need some time to ourselves. So this weekend, while I don't have any scenes to film, we're dropping Katie off at Wes's mother's house and spending those two days together... probably in bed. Between my parents, Wanda, and Andie, Katie has a lot of different people helping to raise her. She's an only child for now, but it's important to us both that she gain a strong appreciation for family. It does take a village, after all.

And after what happened to Andie and me, we're even closer than ever. After I finally got back with my parents and explained in detail what Eddie did, they were so apologetic about not instantly believing me. They begged for my forgiveness, explaining that it wasn't that they were choosing Eddie's side, they were just in shock and feeling so guilty that the man they allowed into their daughters' lives could have done such a thing. Dealing with Eddie in court, being hounded by paparazzi and reporters in the wake of the scandal breaking news in the media, it was all a lot to handle. But I leaned on my family and on Wes to get through that difficult time, and now we are all closer and happier than ever.

In fact, my experience has opened up another door for me. I've become an activist of sorts, visiting schools, giving speeches and spreading awareness about the prevalence of sexual assault and harassment in the entertainment industry. I speak out because I want to give a voice to those who are still afraid to speak for themselves. I want young women and girls coming into Hollywood to protect themselves and for them to have someone to turn to if something bad happens, so they don't feel so isolated and trapped in a bad situation. I've made a lot of good friends through this activism, and even though some people have criticized me for it, I can handle that. I know what I'm doing is right, and my family and the love of my life support me through every step of the way.

"I've just got a few more scenes and then I can head home. Are you gonna wait around for me?" I ask Wes. He nods.

"Of course. Katie's been begging me all week to let her watch you work," he says, grinning. "She's very interested in watching you do your own stunts, apparently."

"Mommy jump!" she squeals happily. I kiss her on the forehead.

"Yep," Wes says. "Your mom is a very talented lady."

"Thanks, love," I tell him. The three of us get up and walk back to the building so I can finish out my work day. As excited as I am to work again, my priorities have shifted a little bit. I work my ass off, but I no longer keep my heart so guarded. I know what truly matters to me now is my family, my happiness. Love is the most important thing in this world. Love anchors me and keeps me smiling through the rough patches, sustains me during long days of filming, and gives me something so beautiful to look forward to when I leave the set every day.

As I film my action scenes this evening, it's all I can do to keep from looking out into the little crowd to find Wes and Katie watching me, both so proud. There was a time when I thought I could never have it all, but I know now that I was wrong. I *can* have it all, and now I do. And while I do love my job, no script I ever read will be as beautiful as my reality.

THANK you so much for reading! I hope you enjoyed <3 If you have a moment, please leave a review. Other readers are dying to know what you thought.

I have plenty more bad boy romance for you, so make sure you check out my other books on the next couple of pages, and sign up for my newsletter to be notified when I have a new release on the way!

~Alexis Abbott

Killing For Her

Abducted

Stepbrothers:

Ruthless

Criminal

Standalones:

Betting on Love

Hunter's Baby

I Hired A Hitman

Vegas Boss

Rock Hard Bodyguard

Innocence For Sale: Jane

Redeeming Viktor

Romance:

Falling for her Boss (Novella)

Most Wanted: Lilly (Novella)

Bound as the World Burns (SFF)

Erotic Thriller:

The Dangerous Men Series:

The Narrow Path

Strayed from the Path

Path to Ruin

ABOUT THE AUTHOR

Alexis Abbott is a Wall Street Journal & USA Today bestselling author who writes about bad boys protecting their girls! Pick up her books today if you can't resist a bad boy who is a good man, and find yourself transported with super steamy sex, gritty suspense, and lots of romance.

She lives in beautiful St. John's, NL, Canada with her amazing husband.

facebook.com/abbottauthor

twitter.com/abbottauthor

instagram.com/alexisabbottauthor

bookbub.com/authors/alexis-abbott

pinterest.com/badboyromance

youtube.com/AlexisAbbott

ABOUT THE AUTHOR

Alexis Abbott is a Wall Street Journal & USA Today bestselling author who writes about bad boys protecting their girls! Pick up her books today if you can't resist a bad boy who is a good man, and find yourself transported with super steamy sex, gritty suspense, and lots of romance.

She lives in beautiful St. John's, NL, Canada with her amazing husband.

facebook.com/abbottauthor

twitter.com/abbottauthor

instagram.com/alexisabbottauthor

bookbub.com/authors/alexis-abbott

pinterest.com/badboyromance

youtube.com/AlexisAbbott

ACKNOWLEDGMENTS

Thank you to my amazing Patrons. I'm constantly humbled and grateful for your support.

Ramona Cabrera
Melissa Hedrick
Virginia Swanson
Dawn Daughenbaugh
Don Doss
Stacie Currie

If you'd like to join them — and get my ebooks or paperbacks — you can find me here on Patreon.
https://www.patreon.com/alexisabbott

www.ingramcontent.com/pod-product-compliance
Lightning Source LLC
Chambersburg PA
CBHW021124190726
48288CB00008B/2493